KING OF THE
CASTLE

KING OF THE CASTLE

A novelisation by Bob Baker

Adapted from the HTV series
by Bob Baker and Dave Martin

fantom
publishing

First published in 2015 by Fantom Films
fantomfilms.co.uk

Quotations from *Childe Roland to the Dark Tower Came*
by Robert Browning

A catalogue record for this book is available from the British Library.
Hardback edition ISBN: 978-1-78196-152-0

Typeset by Xanna Eve Chown
Jacket design by Stuart Manning

Printed and bound in the UK by CPI Group (UK) Ltd
Croydon, CR0 4YY

Contents

Preface

'AH, BOB AND DAVE, could you do us another seven-parter for the children's slot?' said Patrick Dromgoole, HTV's Head Of Programmes.

We said yes, of course, and that was it!

'The contract will be in the post...'

Yet again, HTV, the comparatively tiny Wales and the West Television Company, were willing to stick their necks out and ask Dave Martin and me to provide them with a seven-part serial for children. It was, as were others of this genre, to go out in the five to six o'clock in the evening slot. The Children's Hour. Like the previous serial we'd done, *Sky*, we were given carte blanche as to the subject matter.

The production was under the auspices of executive producer Patrick Dromgoole, and Leonard White, a greatly admired producer we'd worked with on *Pretenders*. Rehearsals began on 13th October 1976 and filming began in early 1977 – a very busy year for us.

As I came to write this novelisation of the serial, I began to wonder about, and tried to remember, the thought processes that David and I had gone through back then. What had led us to arrive at this very strange, dark story? (With a happy ending, of course!)

The roots of it sprung from a long conversation we'd once had with one of the armourers on the battle scenes of *Pretenders*. He had proposed that the exciting world of the Sixties and Seventies that we found ourselves in – the music, the art, the ideas – were, in the main, brought about by something that was fast dying out, owing to the new comprehensive system of education: The Working Class Grammar School Boy. He cited Lennon and McCartney, Peter Nicholls, David Bailey and John Osborne; hosts of film makers, artists, sculptors; and new kinds of actors, such as Albert Finney, who brought a bit of grit to the media. Last, but not least, there was Dave himself, who revelled in his working class Birmingham youth and had been to grammar school and university.

On the face of it, this was a theme that (given our five o'clock programme slot) should have been avoided at all costs! However, it was something we very much wanted to do: a story about a young man's struggle to overcome seemingly insurmountable odds. When we combined this with a headline in the local paper – *Louts Prowl Stairs Of Tower Block!* – it seemed we were getting a story together.

Dave and I went to the tower block in that report to do a bit of research – in broad daylight, I hasten to add! We had a chat with a few people and found their main complaint was that the lift hardly ever worked. It was constantly having to be repaired because of vandals. The landlord, the Bristol Corporation, informed us that the flats were a no-go area at night. A gang stalked the stairs and there were regular fights between rivals. Even the police couldn't cope with it.

A story idea was beginning to gel. Some days later, when we got back from a lunch at our local pub, we sat in the office mulling over the ideas we'd put together. After a silence, Dave suddenly quoted from a poem by Browning: 'Childe Roland to the Dark Tower came.' We started to try and imagine what it might be like for a 'misfit' to live in a block of flats like the one we'd visited.

Yet another story strand came from the fact that several of my friends had gone to the Bristol Cathedral School on singing scholarships. One was the late, lamented, satirical comedian, John Fortune, so I had his experiences to call on. Our Roland, we decided, was to be a chorister who'd just gone through two traumatic experiences. His parents had split up and he'd moved house – a double whammy of life's psychological crises. He was now living on the top floor of a tower block with his father and new stepmother. Roland's struggle with both problems are reflected in his secretive, withdrawn behaviour. Feeling rejected and put-upon, he has lost interest in all but the fantasy world depicted in the sci-fi and horror comics he reads avidly.

And so we had our hero: Roland Anthony Wright, a working-class, grammar-school boy who was totally out of his depth, and unable to deal with the situation he found himself in.

The unspoken norm at the time was that children's programmes should portray a typical family unit of mum and dad plus two or three children. Venturing into broken homes was seen as a bit of a risk. The committee that oversaw such things – the ITV Board – could reject a series because of it. We decided to take that risk, but we needed the support of the producer and HTV.

The next thing which came apparent was that our tale was starting to take on a Kafka-esque feel. Both Dave and I had great admiration for the work of Franz Kafka, whose stories *The Trial* and *The Castle* are filled with themes of alienation; physical and psychological conundrums; parent/child conflict; and characters on a terrifying quest through bizarre labyrinths of bureaucracy and mystical events. All these things had begun to creep into our story! When we typed up an outline, we looked at it and burst out laughing. A Kafka-esque children's serial? They'll never accept it! However, the more we thought about it, the more enthusiastic we became. You can't do Kafka for kids... can you?

We got some very worried looks from producer Leonard White, who told us in no uncertain terms that we were treading on eggshells with this story. But our enthusiasm, coupled with our willingness to stay within guidelines on knives and violence, finally convinced him.

Patrick Dromgoole, executive producer and head of programmes at HTV, would ultimately carry the can, should it be rejected. However, he encouraged us to 'just get on with it' – which was nice.

The result was that, after much haggling and cajoling of the committee, HTV were allowed to go ahead and make *King Of The Castle*.

Production started in late October 1976. We had found our lead, Roland, after exhaustive auditions. He was Philip De Costa and he was supported by an excellent cast: Fulton Mackay, Talfryn Thomas, Milton Johns, Angela Richards, Sean Lynch and Patrick Durkin.

Peter Hammond was to direct the first two episodes. Hammond was an amazing choice, as the piece fitted his style of edgy direction perfectly. Other episodes were to be directed by Leonard White and Terry Harding.

There was stiff opposition to the programme when it was submitted to the network for broadcasting. They had worries, not just about the violence, but the very tenor of the piece. However, all these struggles went on without our knowledge, and the show was finally aired later that year.

I remember a day, not long after, when Dave and I were seeing a producer at the ATV studios in Borehamwood. We were at lunch, when one of the ATV executives we'd met on a previous visit, came over to us, all smiles and compliments. We wondered why...

When we got back to Bristol, there was a message for us to see Patrick Dromgoole and Leonard White as soon as possible. We were highly intrigued, and then delighted, when we finally found that *King Of The Castle* had been nominated for a BAFTA in the category of Best Children's Programme. We didn't win it, however the nomination was a tremendous accolade – and it proved you *could* write Kafka for Kids!

Chapter One

'Childe Roland to the Dark Tower came.'

ROLAND ANTHONY WRIGHT, aged fourteen, a red-haired, freckled schoolboy, emerged from the glass door of a block of flats and ran across the muddy patch of grass towards the bus stop, his satchel thudding against him as he headed for the waiting bus.

Brandon Tower was a block of high-rise flats dating from the Sixties. It stood rigid, upright, like a single finger raised in defiance, amid a surrounding low-rise council house estate.

On that day – Wednesday, September 16, 1976 – Roland felt a measure of victory, since to his surprise and relief the tower block lift had actually been working. This meant that he'd managed to slip out of Brandon Tower with no sight of *them* – the malevolent gang of what his stepmother called 'yobbos'. In other words, the kids that lived in the block who, for no apparent reason, preyed on Roland and seemed to hate, loathe and detest him.

Roland accelerated to reach the green Bristol double-decker bus and just managed to grab the rail on the boarding platform and scramble aboard before it moved off.

He got a hard stare and stern words from the bus conductress, 'You know that's against the law, jumpin' on like that.'

'Sorry,' lied Roland.

As he rode the three miles to the Bristol Cathedral Choir School for Boys, Roland pondered on why the yobbos wanted to rough him up – because that's what they'd threatened, and more besides. It was a train of thought that led to other, darker imaginings. Was it possible, he wondered, that they knew about his mother? Had they found out that it was his fault she and his dad had split up? For Roland was certain he *had* been responsible, although he couldn't put his finger on the actual means he had used...

As his stop approached, he cleared these thoughts away, shut them in a box in his mind – along with other worrisome subjects like exams, his solo piece and the dreadful thought of *girls*. All these were imponderables that could wait until another time. There were other horrors to face before this day was through. This was the very day he was to sing the oratorio solo. Pangs of guilt took hold for a second as he considered it. He knew damn well he hadn't practised it thoroughly.

Roland passed the imposing edifice of Bristol Cathedral, next door to the school. Its history had doggedly remained in his memory ever since he'd had to write an essay on the subject to read aloud in class: *The school dates from 1140. It was originally built as an abbey, but, in 1542, Henry VIII had other ideas. He smashed up all the monasteries and ordered that the abbey be turned into a school. The Bristol Cathedral School.*

The school prided itself on producing choristers for the services held in the cathedral, and it was purely because of Roland's fine soprano voice that he had been granted a place as a scholarship pupil – his academic work left something to be desired. Roland supposed that his musical ability came from his dad, who played the saxophone. Ron was a jazz/rock musician who was often away in the evenings and weekends, doing gigs.

In his classroom, Roland spent a while cleverly concealing a horror comic inside the pages of the very music score he was to perform that day. It was the music he should have paid all his attention to but Roland – being Roland – was well into *Curse Of The Mummy's Tomb* when the eleven o'clock choir bell rang.

As usual, Roland dawdled while putting on his surplice, and half his attention was still on the comic as he trailed after the other boys into the corridor. He joined the chattering double file of choristers as they walked across the courtyard to a low, round-arched door, where the school's music master was waiting.

Mr Hawker was a thin, worn man. He too was wearing a surplice and sported a dark red hair extension, which he confidently supposed went unnoticed by all. He watched the boys in, then focused on Roland, who seemed deep in his music score, bringing up the rear. 'Always one, isn't there, Wright?'

Roland registered that he'd been singled out and used his regular foil to Hawker's sarcasm – pretending that he didn't hear. 'Pardon, sir?'

'Always last, Wright?' Hawker said, with a smug grin. '*Toujours en retard,* Wright, *n'est pas*?'

'Looking at my solo, sir,' lied Roland.

Hawker gave Roland a shove into the cathedral. 'Always wrong forever, Wright.' Smiling to himself, he followed the boys into the cloisters.

The level of their chatter rose at every pace they took.

Hawker placed a protective hand on his hairpiece and hurried on. 'Quiet now, please. Remember where you are.'

This had no effect.

Hawker tried a stentorian shout, 'Silence in the house of God!'

This brought immediate silence.

There was the sudden sound of a loudly slammed door and the choirmaster appeared. Doctor Spurgeon was a pale, frightening, beaky-faced man with a protruding Adam's apple. He stood in his tattered long black gown, arms akimbo, a tall, yet hunched, vulture of a man, and dared anyone to speak. 'Thank you, Mr Hawker,' he said. 'No need of shouting, I am sure.' He turned his beady gaze upon the boys. 'Now, who, *who* might be giving us his solo today, mn?'

The 'mn' was a speech characteristic of Spurgeon's and was copied by Hawker when the choirmaster wasn't around.

The boys all turned their eyes unerringly on Roland.

'Me, sir,' said Roland, with apparent confidence. But he had that nauseous feeling in the pit of his stomach that he always got when performing for his elders.

'Good then,' said Spurgeon. He strode off to the organ stairs and mounted them to take his seat, high upon the great cathedral organ.

Hawker followed him and stationed himself to Spurgeon's left, ready to turn the pages of the music.

During this short time, Roland was able to separate his comic from his solo score without being seen.

Silence was maintained as Spurgeon plunged his talon fingers down on the keys to produce a heavy sombre chord – the prelude to a jagged and difficult piece by Bartok. Spurgeon used the organist's mirror to keep a beady eye on the choir down behind him as he played the introduction.

Hawker turned to the choir and raised his arms with extended forefingers. He nodded and waved his arms for them to start.

As they sang the opening verse, the cathedral was filled with Slavic god-fearing gloom.

Roland was isolated in the centre of the choir stalls as he waited for his intro. He succeeded in slipping his comic into the back cover of the score at the precise moment Hawker was gazing heavenward, but, recklessly, he couldn't resist taking a last, lingering look at it before realising that his solo piece was upon him... Too late, Roland switched his attention to the score and nodded the count into his solo.

Spurgeon slammed down a handful of crashing thunderous chords – the introduction to Roland's solo – but Roland's dulcet tones did not fill the waiting air.

All was quiet for a second or two, then Roland's tremulous note was heard.

Spurgeon brought it to a halt by slamming a massive discord. The silence that followed was eerie, until the apparently calm and amiable voice of Spurgeon cut in. 'Boy! Do try and let the rest of us know when you – mn? – wish to join in. Mn?'

'Sir, sorry, sir.' Roland sounded contrite, but it was only a mask to conceal his dissent.

Spurgeon saw this, but chose to ignore it. 'Again,' he said, in that ever-so-calm voice.

The chords thundered out the prelude to the solo again. Roland came in and was all right for a couple of bars, then his voice started to strain. His control over his voice weakened, producing an ear-piercing discord. It was, unfortunately, a very long note.

Spurgeon stopped playing and allowing the wrong note to go on in the silence, until Roland finally stopped singing.

Hawker shook his head ruefully.

Spurgeon stood, gathering his gown and slammed in a heavy, left-hand chord. 'I am the Wrath of the Almighty!' he said, then turned to look towards Hawker. 'He is my Handmaiden.'

Hawker hid a smile.

'They,' continued Spurgeon, waving at the choir, 'are the Host of Israel. You – mn? – are the Angel of Light.'

The choirboys found this very amusing and giggling broke out in the ranks.

This stopped immediately when Spurgeon screamed, 'That!' He pinged the note repeatedly. 'Is an F natural. Mn?' He suddenly became quiet and menacing. 'Sing it.'

Roland opened his mouth and began to sing the note as Spurgeon descended from his organ eyrie, followed by Hawker who copied his every gesture, perhaps without realising it.

Spurgeon towered over the isolated figure of Roland and spoke over the boy's failing voice. 'I assume that you have made a close and careful study of the piece? Worked hard on it? Practised it? Considered the function of the solo in relation to the whole? But in your wisdom – mn? – you have decided that the composer was wrong, could be improved?' He held his hand up to silence Roland's singing. 'Or could it, might it, could it be your *copy* at fault? Mn?'

As he said this, he delicately picked up Roland's score between finger and thumb, and out fell the horror comic. It hit the stone floor with a splat. Spurgeon looked down at the comic, then screwed up his face in disgust at the lurid cover. It showed a half-naked girl emerging from a sarcophagus, trailing bandages and holding a snake. The banner headline read: *After thousands of years, the Mummy awoke, ravenous for blood to renew her power!*

Spurgeon raised his head, begging for divine disapproval, and pushed a hand through his unruly mane of hair.

Hawker essayed the same gesture, but found his wig in peril and stopped short.

Spurgeon turned a basilisk eye on Roland once more. 'What is your name, boy?'

Roland was to be dressed down in the band room. As he waited to hear his punishment from 'Spurgee', as the boys called him, he gazed at the locked cage which held the expensive brass instruments. There was a shelf full of professional-looking recording equipment, which included recorders, pot earphones, mikes, amps and speakers. A large case for a double bass lay open on the floor – looking not unlike the sarcophagus pictured in his comic.

Spurgeon and Hawker entered the room, Hawker shadowing his mentor and reproducing his every gesture behind his back.

'Now,' said Spurgeon. 'Remind me of the name?'

'Roland Anthony Wright, sir,' answered Roland bravely. He watched as Spurgeon wrote the name down in his black book.

'And you are a scholarship boy?'

'Yes, sir.'

Spurgeon made a flat grin (and just behind him, Hawker reproduced the same grin) as he warmed to his subject. 'So. You came here on a music scholarship. You are receiving the best education in the city for virtually nothing, mn?'

'Yes, sir.'

'No, sir! The school is giving you your education. And you, in turn, are giving us your *voice*.'

'Yes, sir.' Roland's eyes shifted towards the windows. Outside were the sounds of freedom. It was lunch break and the boys were shrieking and shouting outside. Roland wished he was out there with them, but knew he had to suffer the ordeal with Spurgeon first.

Spurgeon split into Roland's thoughts. 'Your attention, boy!'

Immediately, Roland whipped his focus back to his tormentors.

'A dubious privilege for which the cathedral pays you, does it not? Four pounds, mn? Per quarter year?' said

Spurgeon, as he got into his stride. 'Wasted! On this!' He waved Roland's comic in front of him in utter disgust. 'Do you know what a choir is, boy? Mn?'

Roland looked blank.

Spurgeon raised his shoulders (Hawker made a similar movement) and took a deep breath before continuing. 'A choir is a machine, a machine through which the voice of the creator can speak. And when parts of that machine don't work boy, don't work, they can be scrapped! Jettisoned, abandoned, thrown out! Thrown out on the heap from whence they came, mn?'

'Yes, sir,' agreed Roland.

Spurgeon waved the comic in Roland's face. 'Trash. Written by trash and read by trash! Well?'

'Yes, sir,' said Roland flatly. He had decided to use a minimal answer technique in situations like this, ever since he'd found – to his cost – that any sign of dissent made things worse. However, Roland wasn't prepared for what Spurgeon was about to do next.

'This is *my* way with trash, boy!' The music professor tore the comic into strips with a kind of evil pleasure. He stared directly at Roland, a smile building on the side of his face. 'What do you say now?'

'Not my comic, sir.' Roland felt pleased with his answer, but was very careful to maintain the blank look that always kept him reasonably safe. His answer, whilst technically an untruth, was pretty cool, and he had to vigorously suppress the grin that was trying to get out.

They looked at each other.

Downtrodden Roland knew from bitter experience that there came a point where the worm may as well turn as cringe. Punishment was inevitable either way. It was possible that this atom of cool might harness his future strength.

Spurgeon knew that if he were to push the boy past his individual sticking point, it was asking for trouble of some sort or another. 'Is that all?' he inquired, icily.

'Yes, sir,' replied Roland.

'No *apology*?' There was a pause as Spurgeon pushed his face menacingly close to Roland's until they were eye to eye. 'Well?'

Roland shifted himself about under Spurgeon's steady gaze as he wondered how to counter this pressure. He decided on being contrite – just. 'Sir, sorry, sir.'

'You will be,' snapped Spurgeon. As he swept past Roland, towards the door, he rapped out an order to Hawker. 'See to it, Hawker. Something suitable, mn?'

Spurgeon eyed Roland for a last moment before making his exit.

In the long corridor, Roland followed Hawker past the overspill desks along its length. Roland began to feel he'd got off pretty lightly and guessed that Hawker wouldn't mete out too harsh a punishment. Surely, Hawker had a certain sympathy for the weak.

But Hawker was in the position of power and relished in it like a dog with a bone. He half turned to Roland as they marched along the corridor. 'You've let us all down, Roland. Mn?'

'Sir?' answered Roland, using the deaf-ear approach.

'Doctor Spurgeon is a brilliant man. Brilliant. My master as well, you know. *Il maestro.*'

'Sir,' replied Roland. The non-answer, totally neutral.

'Oh, what passes for thought in the blocked and sealed catacombs of your mind? Mn?'

'Don't know, sir.' That should really stump him, thought Roland.

'Yet you're privileged. You've been blessed with a voice.'

In milliseconds, Roland weighed the pros and cons of being blessed with a voice and answered, totally unconvinced. 'Ugh. Yes, sir.'

Hawker led Roland back towards the dinner room. Then felt a further warning was required. 'And remember, once that voice of yours breaks, it's back to work. Homework, schoolwork, full time lessons...'

'I don't mind that, sir,' said Roland, with complete honesty.

This statement was enough to stop Hawker in his tracks. He looked round and muttered with hushed tones. 'What? Do you want to leave the choir? Mn?'

Roland struck this one with the middle of the bat, straight back to him. 'Don't know, sir.' He secretly wished he *could* leave the choir, but he couldn't see a way this could ever happen.

'But Wright, you realise you could lose your music scholarship?' Hawker was quick to remind him. 'End up on Doctor Spurgeon's scrapheap. Mn?'

As they arrived at the kitchen and dining room, they heard the clatter of knives and forks, and the bell that meant dinner was over.

Roland felt a pang of hunger in his stomach and wondered if he would get something in return for missing his lunch. 'Sir?' he said.

Hawker had come to the same conclusion. 'You may have missed lunch.'

'I have, sir.'

They moved on to the staffroom.

Roland was bitterly disappointed at missing his meal. What made it worse was the lingering aroma of meat, two veg, and gravy wafting in the air around him. This too must be borne, he thought, on top of the loss of his comic and the dressing down from Hawker and Spurgeon.

'Wait here,' said Hawker as he went into the staffroom to collect the music that Roland would have to learn. *Punishment* music.

Roland gazed up at the painting above the dinner hall entrance. It depicted Oliver Twist asking for more. He felt that hunger pang again, but he just had to bear it.

Hawker reappeared from the staffroom with a thick psalm book and landed it in Roland's arms. 'You will prepare Dutton's setting of the descant of Psalm 43 for break on Monday,' he said sternly. Then, he looked at Roland's blank face and relented slightly.

Hawker decided to ask a diverting question, one that would help him get a handle on Roland's state of mind. It was an idea that modern teaching methods espoused but, although Hawker knew what *sort* of question to ask, overall this kind of psychology left him completely in the dark. He had no idea how he might deal with Roland's answer, even if it was honest.

He had a go anyway. 'Everything all right at home?'

'Yes, sir. Only we've just moved, sir.'

'D'you like it?'

Roland's mind was a mass of loathing and frustration

over recent events in his life, and especially his new home, but he put them away and allowed his feelings out in a kind of code for those who might understand. 'Top floor in a block of flats, sir.'

Hawker forced a smile. 'Ah well. New faces, new friends, eh?'

'Yes, sir,' said Roland, with a stony glare.

That evening, as Roland approached the imposing tower block, he caught sight of a young boy, smaller than himself, playing with a football.

The boy was kicking it against the wall and then trapping the rebound neatly under his foot. But, as soon as he saw Roland approaching, he picked up the ball and ran into the tower block.

Although Roland guessed that the boy was some kind of lookout for *them,* he had no choice but to continue towards his home, knowing full well what was coming. In preparation, he unshipped his satchel from his neck and held it in one hand with his copper-handled leather music case.

He plodded on towards the entrance and pushed hard on the entry door to get into the foyer. It was entirely empty, but Roland was aware of the sound of feet running up the stairs and a '*Shhhh!*' followed by the sound of excited laughter...

All in anticipation of roughing him up.

To *them,* Roland was an alien. Even if his family was just as poor, they were different. Roland attended a posh grammar school and his father was a musician – not labouring or working at a factory or in an office, but off on tours to the continent. Why, he even probably spoke French!

Roland loved his father, and his father was rightly proud of him. Roland knew he hoped that, one day, his son would become a musician too. But this mattered not one hoot when the gang on the stairs went into hunting mode. After all, for them, Roland was fair game. He was *different*. That meant – in a kind of weird backwards-Darwinian way – the mass were trying to root out those who diverged from the norm. Which meant that, for Roland, there was clear and present danger of painful and unpleasant acts against his person.

And so it began. From the foyer, Roland heard feet running on the floor above as the gang positioned themselves.

Then he heard the voice of Alf, the small boy, shouting, ''Ere he is!'

Roland stopped and looked about warily. He tiptoed to the stairwell and looked up, but there was no one to be seen. He moved over to the lift and pressed the call button, but there was no response from the doors, other than an ugly, metallic graunching noise from above. He heard laughing again and moved back to the stairwell, but he still couldn't see anyone. He decided to try the lift just once more. He pressed it, and this time heard the low buzz of relays straining, trying to operate.

A hand clasped him on the shoulder.

Roland jumped out of his skin, thinking they'd got him. He swivelled around to see the face of Vine the caretaker, a shifty-looking man in his forties, wearing his usual brown overall coat and a collarless shirt topped off by a bent trilby hat. Vine always carried a huge bunch of keys on a ring around his wrist, which he played with constantly.

'What d'you think you're doing?' asked Vine, with a strong South Wales accent.

'Trying the lift,' blurted out Roland.

Vine's eyes narrowed. 'Do you live here?'

'Moved in last week.'

'Oh yes, you're the new lot on the top.' Vine scrutinised Roland, his blazer and badge, then said matter-of-factly, 'Well, it's out of order. You go to grammar school, don't you? Supposed to be intelligent, aren't you?'

Roland showed no emotion.

'Can't you read?' Vine pointed to a tiny message on the lift door, high above Roland's head, written in biro and stuck on with Sellotape: OUT OF ORDER. 'The men are working on it now.'

Roland was suddenly full of hope. This could be his lifeline! 'Will they be long?' he asked, eagerly.

Vine shrugged and laughed. 'You don't think they'd tell me, do you? Nobody ever tells me anythin'.'

'What's wrong with it?' asked Roland. As a last resort, he rashly considered that he might be able to guess how to mend it himself. Things were looking increasingly bleak.

'Hooligans,' snapped Vine. Then he looked above as if he could see through the concrete and said wearily, 'Honest, I don't know what they do up there.'

Roland felt no need to put on any kind of fearful look. Instead he tried to demonstrate that he was not one of *them*. 'Mr Vine, could I use your service lift, please?' he asked, as politely as he could.

Vine sucked through his teeth, as he was wont to do, and slowly shook his head. It was obviously more than his job was worth. 'Sorry, no. The engineers are using it. And anyway it's against the safety rules. All written in the book. One of my ten commandments, you might say.' Vine quoted it verbatim. '"The service lift is strictly for use by the Caretaker and any such person or persons who may have permission to be working in the building or in cases of emergency. Tenants are not allowed to travel in the service lift at any time." Clear enough, eh, boy? Have to make your own way up, won't you?'

As far as Roland was concerned, his situation really was an emergency, but he could see he was fighting a losing battle with Vine.

At that moment, the service lift arrived at the ground floor and the doors swished open. Roland hung around to see what was going on.

Two burly engineers stepped out of the service lift and Vine closed in on them. 'Any luck?' he asked, with the air of someone who hopes the news is bad.

The heaviest of the two, Curry, shook his head and looked pained. 'Not so far, chief. Looks like a whole load of trouble.'

His partner, Hurdle, a real Jeremiah if ever there was one, butted in, 'Right old cag-up.'

Curry shook his head sagely in appreciation of the enormity of the job.

'He could be out all weekend,' said Hurdle.

'All the doors jammed, see,' interrupted Curry.

'Solid,' said Hurdle gravely. 'Use your phone, can we? Only I'll have to ring the boss and tell him.'

Vine was not happy with this request and shifted his feet awkwardly. 'Well, strictly speakin'...'

'Got to tell the Super,' argued Hurdle.

'Can we, then? Use your blower?' asked Curry.

'Give him a tinkle, can we?' said Hurdle.

Vine was reluctant, but knew he was obliged to let them use 'his' phone. 'Well, if you got to. It's in my cubicle.'

The engineers walked off towards Vine's tiny office.

'Ring 03 to get an outside line,' advised Vine as an afterthought.

'Thanks,' said Curry.

'Ta,' said the other.

Vine turned to Roland. 'Well, you heard. Go on, make your own way up.' With that Vine marched off, leaving Roland on his own again.

Roland was back where he'd started. All his hopes of being miraculously lifted out of his terrible situation had gone with the wind. There was nothing for it but to use the dreaded stairs.

He pulled himself together and made his way to the stairs. He started up and successfully found himself on the first floor, but he was terribly aware of something on the next level. He could hear suppressed giggles and footsteps.

He took the bull by the horns and started on the second flight. He was halfway up when three paper waterbombs fell – *Splat!* – around him. One landed on his shoulder. He took out a paper handkerchief and dried his blazer. There was more stifled laughter from above.

Roland strode up the stairs two at a time. He reached the second floor and there was no one to be seen. The unseen gang were still ahead of him.

He passed floor two, and was on his way up to floor three, when half a dozen marbles fell around him, bouncing up high and ricocheting off the walls. He was really scared now. He stopped, wanting to turn back, then forced himself to go up a few more steps.

A wet soggy newspaper filled with the remains of fish and chips, potato peelings and cabbage leaves landed beside him, closely followed by a tin can, then another tin can... and more!

Roland started to retreat under the hail of rubbish but, between the wall and the banisters, he glimpsed the arms and legs of children approaching from below. He was sandwiched between two groups.

Roland decided to race for home. He sprinted up the staircase as fast as he could, passing in turn floors four, five, six, seven, eight and nine...

The sounds of pursuit were closing in on him as an old lady opened her door, about to go shopping. Roland moved towards her, to appeal for help, but when she heard the rumpus and realised what was going on, she slammed her door shut again. Roland ploughed on.

He was on floor ten when the pack caught up with him. Exhausted, he watched the gang approach as he gasped for air. His young neighbours surrounded him. Now they'd covered his escape route, they sat down on the stairs, smiling. They all wore dirty pastel bags, denims and boots.

Out of this mass of humanity stepped the self-proclaimed leader of the pack. He was resplendent in an army jacket, which was covered in all manner of badges and studs – like a Hell's Angel who couldn't afford the leather. On his back the name 'Ripper' was emblazoned in studs.

Ripper gave Roland a superior grin. "Allo, Sunbeam. Heard you was a singer. That right?' He grabbed hold of Roland's music case and opened it, removing a sheaf of music. He took a cursory look at it, then held the sheets over the abyss of the stairwell. 'This your music, is it?'

Roland's heart was beating fast. He had no defence against violence. He could think of nothing to do, other than maybe shooting Ripper in the heart with his laser-bolt eyes, like one of his comic book characters would. *Strang! Laser Killer!* But, of course, he didn't possess such a skill. Wild hopes filled his head. A patrolling copper might suddenly appear and make the gang scatter. His dad might come down the stairs and rescue him. Surely somebody would come to his aid...

Roland watched helplessly as Ripper let go of the music sheets. He looked down the stair shaft and saw them separating and fluttering like migrating wild geese. All he could do was stay quiet. He was employing his usual tactic of appearing detached from the goings on, but inside he wanted to rush at Ripper. Punch him, kick him, scratch him. Didn't the stupid idiot understand what he was doing? That was my homework, Roland thought. If I don't get it done, I'll be *killed*!

As if he knew what Roland was thinking, Ripper began tearing the sheet music into shreds before launching them into the stairwell. He was laughing as he did it, trying hard to get Roland to defend his belongings, so that he could hammer him.

Roland was too scared to move. He was sure that if he cried or protested he would get done over even more – for being a coward.

Ripper looked at the note-covered sheets with something near disgust. He repeated his taunt. 'This your music, is it? This your music?' He jettisoned more sheets. 'This music? Music, is it? This what you sings, is it? This what you goes to that school for?' Ripper emptied the last few sheets out of the case in front of Roland and put his foot on them, scuffing and tearing the paper. 'That's it, then? Your music?' He grinned evilly as he trampled the sheets.

Roland could feel emotion welling up inside him, ready to overflow. He could tell that was about to do something, and whatever it was would be quite involuntary. Kick Ripper in the shins perhaps? Or a quick right hook? He had no idea how or what his retaliation might be. Maybe his tormentor had a glass jaw and would be down and out in a second!

What actually came out of Roland's mouth was one quivering word, 'Don't.'

Ripper smiled, knowing he'd got his quarry riled. He put on a face and silly voice and said, 'Oh, poor little diddums.'

'Leave it,' said Roland. He knew it was his own voice he could hear, but it felt like someone else was speaking.

Ripper kept grinding the music sheets even harder, trying to provoke him further.

The other, involuntary voice came from Roland's lips again, 'Swine!'

This was exactly what Ripper was waiting for. His face went into a scowl. 'What did you call I?' he said, as he grabbed Roland roughly by the lapels.

'Leave me alone then,' said Roland's plaintive voice.

The ring of kids closed in around Ripper and Roland. There was going to be a fight!

Hanging back from the group were two girls, Della and Betty, and with them was little Alf, the lookout.

Roland tried to catch their attention. *I'm helpless. Do something. Please!* he sent by mind transference.

The girls obviously didn't receive the message. They gave him nothing, just looked on – apparently disapproving of the whole situation.

In this weird time-warp situation, Roland's attention came back to Ripper.

Ripper was still waiting on an answer. 'What did you call I?' he insisted.

'Nothing.'

'Who d'you fink you are, eh? 'Cause you ain't. All right, Sunbeam? You're nuffink, all right? Nuffink, see?' He pushed Roland into the ring of spectators. They pushed him back to Ripper, and he continued to provoke him. He grabbed at Roland's pocket and tore it. 'Wha's matter? Cassn't fight?' Roland was shoved around the circle. 'Silly girl's blouse!' shouted Ripper.

Roland noticed the two girls again. They obviously didn't like what they were seeing, but still they did nothing.

Little Alf shouted to them, 'Ripped his coat, look!'

Ripper pushed Roland so that he staggered back towards a wall resplendent with garish spray-on graffiti. Ripper grabbed a handful of Roland's hair and held him under the part of the wall art which claimed *Ripper Rules OK.*

'See? See that? That's me. All right? When you wants to come up these stairs, you asks me. And you asks me nice... Got it, Sunbeam?' He suddenly let go of Roland.

There was somebody coming up the stairs.

It was Vowles, the council worker in charge of care and

maintenance at the flats. He was wearing a Mac and carrying a briefcase. Roland remembered meeting him when they had moved in. Would he now be Roland's saviour?

'Come on, there's good lads,' Vowles said. 'Let's get past. Some of us have got work to do. It's your lift you know, not mine. I only work here.'

Roland noted that Vowles was intimidated by the gang, and remained carefully neutral when he spoke to them.

The gang barely moved in response, so that Vowles had to force his way through. On his way through, he glanced down at Roland, who was trying to retrieve a few sheets of tattered dirty music, but passed by without comment.

Roland knew full well that Vowles was aware of what was going on. Assault, that's what it is, thought Roland, so why didn't he do anything to stop them? Scared, I suppose. Just like I am...

Vowles squeezed through the circle of youths, and even gave them a weak smile. 'Thank you now, thank you,' he said as he passed through and out into the corridor and on to the next staircase. As he pushed past Alf and the girls, the best thing he could think of was to shake his head in mild reproof.

When Vowles had gone, Ripper returned to his threatening, belligerent self. 'See?' he said. 'Now you ask.'

After a slight hesitation, during which he entertained thoughts that he might soon be free to go, Roland said in a quaking voice, 'Let me go up the stairs.'

A raised fist and glare from Ripper. He went up close to Roland's face and yelled, 'Properly!'

Roland's head was spinning, wondering quite what he meant. He opted for, 'Please...'

Ripper didn't move and kept his foot on Roland's music.

Roland tried again. 'Please can I go up the stairs, please?'

Ripper lifted his foot from the music, which was now crumpled and dirty with boot marks. He grinned, victorious. 'Yeah, all right.'

As Roland moved away, Ripper gave him not so much a kick but a shove with his boot.

Roland entered his bedroom. It was very bare and somewhat unfriendly looking, with the 'bomb site' feel of one who had recently moved. All his toys, books and knick-knacks lay in two un-emptied tea chests in the middle of the room. Roland hadn't yet had the time, or the inclination, to make the room his own.

He threw himself on his bed with his satchel and music case, then turned and pushed his face into his pillow so that his parents wouldn't hear his sobbing.

Above him, two posters in a vaguely Tolkien style had been hastily taped to the wall: one showing knights in armour fighting on a castle stairway, the other with the castle in the background.

In the living room, Roland's father had large 'pot' headphones on and was listening to some music on a big, new Sony stereo tape recorder. He was engaged in transcribing an arrangement for his band. He listened to a phrase, stopped the machine, wrote it down on a music sheet, then started again. It took up all his concentration.

Ron was forty-one, a big man with long dark hair and the beginnings of a salt-and-pepper beard. He worked at British Aerospace for a living. Full stop.

Despite his day job as a technician, Ron's world lay firmly in music. He was a gifted musician who had discovered rock via dance bands and jazz, and now belonged to Gas Attack, an outfit (as he insisted on calling them) that played hard rock, verging on heavy metal. They played gigs nearly every night of the week and it had been mooted that they should go fully professional. However, Ron preferred to keep the anchor of his well-paid job.

Ron came from a solid working class, non-conformist Methodist background and was one of a few in his area who had attended a grammar school – the archetypal working class grammar school boy. He had been delighted when Roland had passed his scholarship exams and followed in his father's footsteps. However, Ron's recent conversion to rock'n'roll had sent him into denial of his 'hardworking man in aerospace' persona. Despite his age, he felt himself part of the Seventies 'youthquake' and was loving it. He had turned into a bit of a hippie, taking on all the trappings of contemporary stars – wearing fashionably ragged clothes, becoming a member of CND, letting his hair grow long and unruly, and maybe even trying the odd drug. Consequently, he had little time for anything else.

June walked into the room. She was Ron's second wife, a short, tidy, attractive woman in her late thirties. She'd been the PA to a director at a local cigarette factory before her marriage, but was now looking after Ron and getting to know her newly-acquired stepson, Roland – a job she felt might last some time!

She looked around the room, taking in the lounge with its cushion-floor lino – a reddish pink design based on French floor tiles. She had done her best to make it look like home. There were some scattered rugs in shades from red to purple, and a tall lamp with a red shade. Three walls were painted white and the fourth had a pale red pattern, based on the signs of the zodiac. There was a gold sunburst convex mirror to make the room look larger. Against the walls was a Thirties-style bureau and a sideboard. In the centre stood a circular white dining table with three white wire chairs and, on it, a glass ball with a falling snow scene. On the floor were three large cushions, the sort you lie on. There was no television set, but a middle sized Rigonda stereo and speakers. On the mantelpiece were June's six Dresden-type china figurines, with two pictures on the wall above, reproductions of Dutch interiors. Somewhere, in amongst Ron's clutter, was a Sixties Brutalist-style Scandinavian three-piece suite.

June went into the kitchen. She turned a gas tap up and called through the serving hatch. 'Ron? Roland's home, love.'

Ron looked through the hatch at her, but that was all. He was still listening intently to his music.

'Love? Roland's in. In his room.'

He figured out what she'd said. 'Oh yeah.'

'You are going to tell him? About his room? Those tea chests have been there a week.'

Instead of replying, Ron picked up his alto saxophone and tried out a phrase he's been working on. It sounded like he was replying to her in music.

'I can't keep cleaning around them.'

In reply she got another tootle.

'Ron!' she called, not too irate.

'Why don't you tell him, love?' said Ron patiently.

'Oh, love, I don't want to sound like I'm nagging.'

Ron took in a breath. 'Look, love, we've been married long enough for you to speak to the lad...' Ron's mind was still obviously elsewhere, somewhere in between the notes in the drone zones of his brain. 'Eh?'

'It's not fair, love. Why should I be the one nagging him all the time? You could show a bit more interest, Ron.'

'What d'you mean? Show more interest? I'm his father!' Ron realised he may have hurt his wife's feelings and backtracked. 'I didn't mean it like that, love.'

'Well I'm not his mother, am I?' she said, with a sad smile. 'What affection will he have if I keep going on at him? That's all I meant, love.'

Ron felt slightly guilty. He had a horror of these confrontations, where one was supposed to be honest and expose feelings that both parties would prefer remained inside, so he relented. 'All right, I'll tell him. Just finish this first.'

June smiled at him, then went off on her own hobbyhorse: astrology. 'Always difficult with Capricorns and Scorpios, anyway.'

'Yes, love,' said Ron.

June smiled to herself at having won a little victory on the road to the happiness she wanted in the family. She looked down at her *Woman* magazine, opened at the astrological predictions page, and read loudly so that Ron could hear. 'It says here that it's a good day for Roland to make new relationships and consolidate old ones.'

'Oh yeah?' Ron answered.

June sighed, realising she would have to see Roland herself.

*

In his bedroom, Roland was standing quite still, apparently sad and moody, looking out of his window at the world below... He suddenly swung around, wielding a bamboo cane about three feet long. He was holding it two handed, in the manner of a Japanese Samurai warrior. He swiped his way around the room, felling imaginary enemies and acting out his aggression.

He dived on to the bed, and smashed his fists into the pillow with a series of punches, cowboy style, and then wrestled with it. Finally, he punched the pillow across the room with a solid thud. Roland's imaginary honour was satisfied. He'd vanquished 'Ripper'.

He pondered on what could he could follow that with.

He moved to one of the tea chests and plucked out a few old comics and a pair of football boots. Then his eyes caught on something further down inside the chest. He pulled out a plastic light-up model of Frankenstein's monster, examined it carefully, and checked the battery was still there. He placed it on his bedside table and turned it on. The eyes of the monster went *flash... flash... flash!*

There was a knock on the door, and Roland snapped out of his reverie.

'Tea's ready love,' came June's voice from outside.

'Coming!' he replied.

Roland opened the door to find June still standing there.

Her eyes darted into his room and the tea chest. 'Oh! You unpacking, Roland?'

He just stared at her.

'Can I come in a minute?' she asked with a warm smile.

He started to resist. 'Well I –'

June gently pushed past him and immediately saw the ripped and dirty sheet music and torn blazer. She went to him and put her arm around his shoulders. 'Oh my God, Roland. Whatever happened? Oh *love*...'

He turned away from her.

She let him go and picked up his blazer. It was more practical, easier to deal with. Her voice was full of concern. 'What's all this? What have you been doing?

In the kitchen, Roland's father faced him with a worried look. 'What d'you mean "Only the pocket"? We don't spend twenty quid on a blazer for somebody to rip. Who was it? Who are they?'

'That lot on the stairs. The lift's out again.'

'What were they doing?'

'Chasing me. Trying to be funny, that's all.'

'Funny? Your mother and I aren't laughing.'

'You should see what they did to his music,' said June. She showed Ron the crumpled sheets. 'They threw the rest of it down the stairs, love.'

Ron showed more anger over the music than the blazer. 'What? This is disgusting, terrible!'

'Go on, go and get it, what's left of it,' said June, as she guided Roland to the door. As Roland went out, she turned to Ron. 'Well love, what're you going to do about it?'

Ron skilfully sidestepped this. He looked at his watch and proclaimed, 'Oh hell! The gig's in half an hour. Still, we ought to do something...'

June scrutinised the tear on the blazer pocket and considered whether she might be able to repair it.

Ron got his stuff ready for his gig. He didn't notice that

Roland had returned with a pile of mucked-up sheet music.

June went on a rant. 'When I think of what we went through to even get this place! Dragging round the council offices day after day. Forms for this, forms for that! I thought at least we'd end up with somewhere decent, not stuck up here with a load of hooligans.'

'And what was that caretaker doing? Can't he keep control?' said Ron.

June joined Roland and took a pile of dirty, crumpled music to show Ron. 'Just look at this, Ron.'

'No good now, Role?' asked Ron. He looked at Roland, becoming more sympathetic.

'No, dad,' replied the boy. He loathed being called Role, although he'd never told anyone. It was such a babyish name, like his dad still thought he was just a little kid.

Ron placed his hand on Roland's shoulder. 'How many were there, son?'

'About ten.' He shrugged, as if to say: there's nothing we can do about it.

'Ten to one?'

'Well it was this big kid really.'

'Well I hope you had a good go at him, Role? Stuck up for yourself, didn't you?'

Roland was taken aback at his father's attitude. He struggled to say anything.

June came to his aid. 'Wouldn't do any good, love. Not with a gang of 'em.'

'I s'pose you just let him do it?' said Ron.

Roland was fighting back tears. What did his father expect of him against Ripper and his gang?

'I told him not to...' Roland tailed off.

June again came to the rescue. 'You come and have your tea, Roland.' She led him off to the kitchen.

Ron stood, irresolute. 'Shall I...?'

There was no reply.

'I'll be getting on then,' said Ron. He packed his saxophone into its case and went into the bedroom.

June served Roland a colourful plate of food that included bright red tomatoes, yellow sweetcorn, orange Saveloys and golden chips. Comfort food. 'Hope it's all right love?' she asked, as she flitted around him assiduously. Now, she thought, this was a chance to get to know him better. 'I got some of that new cordial you might like to try? Makes a change from just orange, eh?' She proffered a bottle of cordial for Roland's approval.

Roland scanned the label, which claimed it was full of Vitamins and Mixed Summer Fruits. He didn't react.

June poured him some.

'Thanks... June.' Roland was hesitant to call her anything other than June. His father had tried to insist that he call her 'mum' but, seeing Roland's sullen reaction, immediately modified his edict to: *try* to call her mother or mum. Roland found it difficult, and for the time being had decided to go on calling her June.

Ron came into the kitchen all done up for his gig. He was wearing tattered jeans and a bright, well-worn, maroon jacket with gold buttons and braid.

June went over to him and brushed some fluff off his sleeve.

Ron looked over at Roland, who was scoffing his food avidly. 'So the lift's out of order, right, Role?' he asked.

Roland answered whilst still chewing, 'Men are working on it.'

A cloud passed Ron's face. He shook his head and looked at June. 'Only I'll need a hand to shift the tools.'

There he goes again, thought Roland. Why 'tools'? Maybe it was Ron's wish to remain un-aloof, to be part of the seething masses of working people – 'equipment' became simple 'tools'... It seemed daft to Roland.

Then came what Roland feared.

'You'll have to give me a hand, son.'

'Ron,' said June with a warning tone.

'He's got to go down sometime.'

'Well, let the poor love finish his tea, will you?'

Roland emerged from the front door, onto the corridor outside their flat, carrying a music case, a folded music stand and a plastic shopping bag full of mikes, wires and plugs.

Ron followed him out, carrying his alto and soprano sax cases. He kissed June firmly on the mouth. 'Bye then, love,' he said.

'What time will you be back?' she asked anxiously.

He shook his head and sounded apologetic. 'Not before three, love.'

June's face dropped. 'Oh... All right,' she said. 'Bye.' Then she turned to Roland. 'You come straight back up, mind.'

Ron headed for the stairs. 'Come on, Role.'

June watched them go, then closed the door.

There was a clatter of footsteps on the stairs as Roland and his dad hurried down to the ground floor.

Ron kept up with Roland, who seemed to be out to beat the world record for descending stairs. He tried to give Roland some cheer. 'Look son, if we see any of this lot, you point him out to me, right?'

But there was nobody about. Floor after floor was completely empty.

More stair clattering and they arrived at the ground floor. They took a quick look around. Nobody there either, but Ron had noticed a crumpled piece of sheet music on the floor. He tutted at it and moved over to the foyer area.

Vine was watching them from his cubicle.

As they went through the front door, they met up with another musician in a similar customised jacket to Ron, who'd been waiting for them.

'Sorry, man. Not late are we? Lift's knackered again, see.'

'Yeah, bit,' said the musician, and took the gear from Roland.

Ron turned to Roland. 'Thanks mate, really appreciate your help.' He looked up at the tower block following Roland's anxious gaze. 'You'll be all right,' he said, optimistically. 'Cheers then, Role. See you tomorrow. Yeah, you'll be all right.'

Roland watched his father get into the waiting VW van and slide the door shut. He waved, rather pathetically, as the van drove off then turned to go back to the flats.

Suddenly a voice came from the shadows. 'That your father, is it?'

Roland, already a bit hyper, practically jumped out of his skin. Then, he realized it was Vine who'd been lurking in the shadows of the doorway, watching Ron's departure.

'Musician is he?' said Vine, with what Roland detected as contempt.

'Yes. Is the lift working yet, please?'

'No,' said Vine, with a modicum of pleasure. 'Going up again are you?'

'Yes,' said Roland.

'Good,' mumbled Vine. He felt in his overall pocket, which was full of keys and various tools. He produced a pair of pliers, a screwdriver and a Stanley knife – the large sort, with a retractable blade, which appeared to be well used and was taped up with insulation tape. He held out the tools to Roland. 'The lift engineers left these down here and they'll be needing 'em. They're on the tenth floor.'

Roland wasn't happy about it, but could think of no way out.

'Don't mind do you? Save my legs!' added Vine, with a weak, toothy grin.

Roland had no option. He took the tools and put them in his pocket.

'Good lad. Do with a few more like you round here. Make my job a lot easier, it would.'

Then, as Roland started off towards the stairs, Vine addressed him more officially. 'Oh, by the way...'

Roland stopped and turned.

'Tell your father, that's a no parking area. All right?'

Roland went up the staircase as quietly as he possibly could, making each footfall practically soundless. Taking each stair one at a time, he moved up through the dark, shadowy floors, one by one, until he reached the tenth floor.

He moved to the lift. The doors were open, but there were no workers to be seen. He walked to the end of the tenth floor landing and still saw nobody. He returned to the lift and saw the now large notice, informing him that the lift was OUT OF ORDER.

Roland called out, sotto voce, 'Hello?'

He got no response, so he called louder, 'Hello?'

Again no response.

He put his head inside the lift, 'Hell-o?'

He hadn't noticed that Ripper and two of his henchmen had appeared behind him and felt another shock to his system, as he heard a mocking voice reply.

''Allo, Sunbeam,' said Ripper. 'What you doin' 'ere?'

Roland moved away from the lift and ran for the stairs, but he was cut off by one of Ripper's mates. He turned, and found himself face to face with Ripper again.

'You're on *my* corridor. You bin walkin' on *my* stairs.'

'The caretaker asked me...' Roland said lamely.

Ripper moved a step closer to Roland and glared directly, malevolently, into his eyes. 'I don't care what that dumbo did. You should have asked me. *Me.*'

Roland backed away until he hit the wall.

Ripper closed in on him, then prodded him hard in the chest. 'Shouldn't you, Sunbeam? Eh? Shouldn't you?'

Roland shouted as firmly as he could, 'Leave me alone!' His hand went to his pocket, to show Ripper the tools Vine had given him. They all fell out onto the floor – except the Stanley knife, blade already out. He grasped the handle. 'Let me *go*!' he said, in a kind of helpless last-ditch reaction.

Ripper backed away in sudden fear. 'Watch out – he's carrying!' he warned his mates.

Roland was too surprised by himself to move.

It gave Ripper and his mates time to recover themselves.

'Go on, Rip! Get 'un, Rip!' urged Buzz, one of Ripper's cohorts.

'What?' said Ripper. He was loath to get his own knife out, but sensed that he was being pushed into it.

'Go on!' yelled Buzz. 'Get 'im!'

Ripper saw no way out without losing face, so he plunged his hand into his pocket and produced his own knife, a switchblade. This got him back to thug status again. 'You made the first move, Sunbeam,' he said with suitable menace. He turned to his mates. 'You saw it, didn't you?'

Both of them shouted, 'Yeah! Go on, Ripper!'

'I got witnesses, see,' said Ripper. He opened up the blade.

'Leave me alone!' shouted Roland in quivering voice.

'You started it!'

They were, in fact, both terrified.

Down below, at street level, car lights swept the building as a police panda car came to a halt at the entrance to the flats. Two men got out and knocked on Vine's door.

'Oh,' said Vine, startled, as he opened it.

'Mr Vine?' inquired Sergeant Tarr.

'Yes. Caretaker,' said Vine.

'People on nights complaining about noise on the stairs. We shall have to have a look.'

Vine shook his head bitterly. 'Nobody tells me anything, see.'

Sergeant Tarr and PC Briggs moved off towards the lift.

Vine moved quickly to overtake them and inform them

that the lift was out of order. 'Use the service lift. That one's out.'

He pressed the call button on the service lift.

On the tenth floor, Roland was still against the wall. Ripper was moving in on him, his mates hanging back to keep watch.

'Let me go,' begged Roland.

'You started it,' said Ripper. He feinted a slash with his blade, well out of range.

Probably just for the benefit of his buddies, Roland thought. He had begun to realise that his tormentor had to escalate the situation, in order to keep face.

'Come on. Come on, Sunbeam! You started it, didn't you? See who finishes it.'

Roland sniffed, close to tears. 'I didn't mean it.'

'Didn't you?' Ripper made a lunge.

A sudden shout from Buzz, 'Coppers!'

The two policemen and Vine came out of the service lift and began to take a look around. They heard footsteps around the next corner and caught site of Ripper and his mates disappearing down the staircase.

Roland was still petrified – and still holding the Stanley knife.

'Stay with him,' ordered Sergeant Tarr to a startled Vine.

Roland saw Vine coming, dropped the knife and made a run for the passenger lift, which still had the doors wide open.

Without thinking, Roland ran into the lift. To his shock and surprise, the main light went out, the doors closed and the lift dropped. Just as if had been waiting for him.

Vine rushed to the lift and jabbed the call button as the two policemen came back. PC Briggs had Ripper by the scruff, frogmarching him.

'I told him!' insisted Vine. 'I *told* him the damn lift was out of order. He ran straight past me.'

'Then what?' asked Sergeant Tarr.

'It went down and he's gone down with it.'

'You mean it dropped? With the kid inside it?' said Sergeant Tarr, a bit concerned.

'No, no, no. It hasn't dropped exactly – but it's gone right down. Right down to the bottom and I can't call it back. It's stuck down there.'

Roland and the lift went down, plummeting with a whooshing sound as the lift accelerated. Roland was in a half-delirious state as he watched the floor indicator lights came up on the indicator panel.

Five... Four... Three... Two... One... Ground... Basement... Lower Basement...

But still the lift went on down, down, down.

Light faded to green dimness, still with the unreal echoey sound of the lift falling, until suddenly it slowed, and then bumped to a halt.

Chapter Two

Into that ominous tract which, all agree,
Hides the Dark Tower. Yet acquiescingly
I did turn...

ROLAND WAS COMPLETELY UNSURE of where, or even when, he was. If he was alive or... What? Was this death? Was he *dead*? If he were, he thought, it seemed quite a bit like being *not* dead...

He was in a strangely calm state. He was not afraid. He'd read of parallel time streams, of out-of-body experiences, of the afterlife... He began to think that perhaps he was in some kind of interim state, waiting for his sins to be considered before being taken into God's heaven – or the other place! The only thing he was sure of was that he was part of *something* on-going, and that soon he would hopefully be able to connect it to his previous life-stream...

Roland got up from the floor slowly, still dazed. He leaned against the lift wall for a second or two, trying to get his bearings as he struggled to understand his plight.

As he sifted through his thoughts, the lift doors slowly opened, revealing what Roland suspected was a dungeon. The place had a buckled, sloping floor. It was stone-vaulted, yet organic in feel, with tree roots twining in and out through the stone. The walls were wet and dripping, smooth too – obviously eroded by water over time. Misshapen iron rings were fastened to the walls and there were trailing cobwebs everywhere. Providing the light was a burning pitch brand on the wall. Ahead of him was an arched, heavily barred wooden door.

'What is this place?' he wondered, but was at a loss to even try to figure out what had happened. It seemed like an imaginary world. It was how he imagined Alice must have felt in that famous rabbit hole, before she got to Wonderland. Like her, he felt he had little choice but to proceed somewhere, and see where it took him.

Roland had a quick look around again, then began to move unsteadily out of the lift and, very tentatively, on into the dungeon.

No sooner than he was out of the lift, than the doors clanked shut behind him. He whirled around, but could see no doors any more, no lift – just another stone wall that blended in with the rest.

He was about to examine the wall when he was distracted by the sound of footsteps dragging up the corridor outside the heavy door. He heard the clink of a key being fitted into the lock and prepared himself for something horrific to appear – some nightmarish figure, a grisly human construct, a zombie, or a flesh eating reptilian ghoul – as the lock went *click!*

There was the noise of a bolt being pulled back and a latch lifting. Roland watched as the door slowly opened with a loud creaking noise. He could do nothing but stare...

Roland's heart quickened when he saw the figure who'd opened the door. The man standing there bore a strange similarity to Vine, but a slightly wizened version. His face was pasty white and his hair longer and blacker. He was wearing a mildewed greenish tailcoat and trousers with elastic bands round the ankles, pointed shoes, and a yellowed wing collar. The outfit was topped off by a mangled silk 'topper' hat. He carried a huge bunch of heavy iron keys, hanging from a chain beneath his coat.

'From above are you?' he said, hardly looking at Roland, in a voice which resembled Vine's.

Roland was not sure how to answer, but blurted out, 'They were chasing me. I was going down in the lift. It wouldn't stop and I...'

'You've ended up here.' Vein cast a beady eye over Roland.

'How far down am I?' Roland felt that this would be a relevant question in one set of circumstances – in a normal world – but in this netherworld, it felt like a silly one.

Vein sucked his teeth and replied, 'Ever so far.'

Roland looked back at where the lift had been. 'How do I get back up?'

'You'll have to make your own way. Up and up and up,' Vein said, squinting at the ceiling. 'Ever so far.'

'What is this place?' demanded Roland, his voice quavering a little.

'Can't you see?' said Vein, crossing over to the ring and chain on the wall, and tugging at it to see if it was still in firmly. 'You're in the dungeon, boy. Deep, deep in the Castle.'

'What castle?' said Roland.

'The Castle. Where else, boy?'

'I don't understand,' said Roland, now very confused.

'Then you must find out.'

Still utterly confused, Roland frowned at Vein. 'Who are you?'

'Don't you know?'

Roland shook his head.

'I am the steward of the keep. The holder,' he rattled his bunch of keys, 'of the keys.' He held them up in front of the boy, enjoying his moment.

Roland calmed himself and looked directly at Vein. 'Can you get me out then?'

Vein grinned.

Roland could almost see the words 'you poor fool' written on his face. He wondered if a bit of crawling might aid him. 'Can you, please? Let me out, please?' he tried.

'Oh no. Can't do that,' said Vein, with a smile on the side of his face.

'Why not?' asked Roland in a more commanding voice, showing a bit of frustration.

Vein lowered his voice and laid a hand on Roland's shoulder. 'There's things... Things needed from you. Things you must do. That's why you're here, Master Roland.'

Roland pulled away from Vein, taken aback. 'How do you know who I am?'

'It's my business to know. We all have names. Names we

are called, names we deserve, and names we don't like. My name is Vein. Names are like keys, boy. They let you know what might... or what might not... lie within.'

'And you say you're called Vein?'

'Mr Vein, yes, if you don't mind. That's V. E. I. N. As in throat,' he added with a brief, sinister smile.

Roland was beginning to feel a bit worried. Not out-and-out scared, but his thoughts were all churning in his mind because he was unsure of what to expect. 'What do I have to do to get out, Mr Vein?'

'To get out, you have to go up, and go up... You have to earn the right key. Come here.'

Roland followed Vein to the dungeon door and watched him unlock it with a huge key.

With a beckoning nod of his head, Vein stepped out into the corridor. 'Follow me,' he said.

Roland watched him go out of sight around a curve in the corridor and wondered if he *should* follow him. He knew he had little option but to do so. After a last, long look at where the lift should have been, he moved out into the long, dark, curving corridor. It was like a labyrinth, with side passages here and there, and flaming pitch brands giving a little spluttering light along the tunnel.

Roland reached a section where there were carved stone faces, heads, and arms sticking out of the wall. He avoided the outstretched arms and kept his eyes away from the more gruesome looking carved heads.

He suddenly saw Vein up ahead of him, beckoning Roland to follow him.

'Where are we going?' said Roland.

'Sssssh!' hissed Vein.

Roland lowered his voice to a whisper. 'Where are you taking me?'

'We're going towards it now.'

'Towards what?' cried an increasingly frustrated Roland.

There was a deep indrawn breath from Vein. 'D'you think they'd tell me? Do you? They never tell me anything!'

Roland turned and asked, 'They? Who are they?'

But Vein was not there. He had completely disappeared and Roland only heard the echoing sound of his voice: *You'll find out... soon enough... soon enough...*

Roland, alone and frightened in the dark corridor, shouted at Vein in vain. 'Mr Vein? Mr Vein! Where are you?'

There was no reply.

Roland became more bold. He took a flaming firebrand from the wall to light his way but, as he moved on, he was accompanied by weird slithering sounds. There were whispering noises, creaks and groans, and the echoes of far off laughter, which got more and more scary as it built in intensity, faded away, and then started again.

Roland's response was to speed up, hurrying as fast as he could along the dank, cobwebbed corridor, while the flaming light threw strange animated shadows in front of him. He noticed that the further he went, the narrower the corridor became, until, finally, he was having to make his way awkwardly around the stone sculptured heads and their outstretched arms. His heart was beating hard and fast through fear and exhaustion.

Then, to his horror, he saw two huge eyes up ahead, glowing in the darkness. He panicked with fright and tried to go back the way he'd come, but the walls began to close over, sealing him off from any escape. The noises behind him began again, but now the corridor was closed off, there was only one way to go...

On went Roland, towards the pair of glowing eyes. He thrust the firebrand in front of him, to give light and a certain protection. He had learned from one of his comics that animals didn't like fire.

Suddenly, he heard a tremendous animal roaring sound. Despite his fear, he considered what he might do. Then, taking a deep breath, he hurled the firebrand into the darkness in front of him.

This action – a positive move – brought about a strange result. It seemed that, having 'taken arms against a sea of troubles', Roland had, by opposing, ended them. He noticed, with some relief, that the creepy noises had stopped. The torch flared up and lit the way ahead, and he saw the eyes again. This time, he looked more carefully, and realised that they were jewelled eyes in a carved stone gargoyle, reflecting the light of the torch – and that the gargoyle was nothing but a fancy door knocker.

Feeling calmer, he looked down and saw an iron key on the stone floor.

Roland took a while to consider it, before deciding to pick up the key. First, he checked behind him, thinking that Vein might be up to something. Then, he looked at the heavy, rough cast key, unsure of what he should do next.

He turned, grasped the ornate gargoyle's head knocker and rapped on the door. It made an empty, hollow, booming noise. He waited, wondering if he should try the key, but decided to knock on the door again.

A sliding panel in the door clicked open and Roland was confronted by Vein's eyes peering out at him.

'Use the key!' said Vein irritably, then snapped the panel shut.

Roland hefted the heavy key in his hand and put it into the lock. He turned the key and swung the heavy door open.

Vein was waiting for him, just inside the door, wearing a grimace that suggested he was none too pleased with Roland's intelligence. He held his hand out for the key to be returned. 'Thank you,' he said sharply, as he grabbed the key from Roland's hand.

'I don't understand,' said Roland pathetically.

'I can see that,' replied Vein with a sour note in his voice. He gave Roland a shove towards a curtained off entrance. 'Now go on.'

Roland held back against the shove, unwilling to venture on without knowing what might lay ahead. 'But what's in there?'

'You want to get out, don't you?' said Vein, who'd become sympathetic all of a sudden. 'Who knows, you might even find a second key. Go on, Master Roland.'

Roland took a step towards the curtain.

'Our man of knowledge is waiting,' stated Vein.

Roland turned to ask more questions, but Vein had vanished into thin air again. Seeing no better option, Roland tentatively parted the curtains and stepped through.

He found himself on a gallery with a flight of steps to the floor. He looked down, and saw a circular shape with arched cloisters of organic form. In the middle were some laboratory benches crowded with glass retorts, all bubbling and smoking away. The centrepiece was a slab on a rostrum, above which hung two large silver spheres. Every now and then, sparks flew across from one sphere to the other with lightning flashes and a loud crackling noise. Close by them was a large iron cage...

As Roland slowly descended the stairs he began to feel that there was something a little familiar about the place. Maybe it echoed the gongs and sound equipment he had seen in the school music room? But he allowed the idea to drift away – he had no time to figure out what or why.

As he reached the floor, he saw various haphazard cables, clamps and wires that connected the spheres to the slab. The slab had manacles for wrists, arms and neck, and behind it was a battery of control instruments.

'Hello? Anybody here?' Roland called out. He wandered over to the benches and equipment. Just as he reached the twin spheres, a spark leapt across with a loud crackling noise, scaring him half to death. At that moment, he caught a glimpse of a figure behind a pillar...

As the light from the lightning flash died away, the room became dark and shadowy again. There was a rustling sound. Roland looked up and caught another fleeting glimpse of a man. He knew he was being watched. 'Who is it? Who's there?' he called.

The only answer was a creaking, squeaking sound like an old wheeled trolley, as the figure continued to spy on Roland, flitting from pillar to pillar.

Roland unwillingly joined the game of hide-and-seek.

The man had the upper hand, watching every move that Roland made and then making his own move, always to end up behind him.

Roland, thinking he would be clever, stepped backwards between two pillars, only to find he was suddenly collared by the man. He twisted around and saw that his captor bore a certain resemblance to Doctor Spurgeon, the choir master. He was wearing a black apron over a flowing white shirt, black waistcoat and trousers of the Lister/Pasteur era.

'You. What's your name boy?'

'Roland Anthony Wright, sir.'

'And are you a scholar, mn?'

'Yes, sir.'

'So. You have come to me for knowledge, mn?'

'Yes, sir.'

'Who sent you? Tell me who sent you.'

Roland unsure at first, then remembered, 'Vein. Mr Vein. He said I would find the man of knowledge.'

The man, Hawkspur, gave a disapproving twitch of his face. 'Vein... Not to be trusted, that man. What else?'

'He said you would help me find a key?'

'Key? What key?' said Hawkspur. He glared straight into Roland's eyes with a glittering hypnotic stare, then went on matter-of-factly, 'You are to forget all about keys. You are here to help me, boy. You understand?'

'I understand,' said Roland, mesmerised by Hawkspur's glare.

Hawkspur let him go. 'Not clumsy are you? In any way shape or form?'

'No, sir.'

'Or deficient? Thoughtless? Forgetful?'

'No, sir.'

Hawkspur's eyes narrowed. 'Deceitful?'

'No, sir.'

Hawkspur paused and thought over his next question. 'Can you sing?'

'Yes, sir,' said Roland, able at last to give a positive answer.

'Good.' Hawkspur seemed to savour the answer. 'Good.'

He led Roland over to the bubbling retorts and flasks, taking him from one set-up to another. 'This is the primordial soup... And this is the basic plasma. Mn?'

'Sir?'

Hawkspur attended to the tap of a retort and said, 'You wish to ask a question?'

'Yes, sir. What am I doing here?'

'Learning!' said Hawkspur. The doctor turned his attention to fiddling with a valve on a minute tap.

Roland wandered over to the slab with its sinister looking manacles. 'Sir? What's this for?'

Hawkspur looked up and replied with a disturbing note in his voice, 'What does it look as if it's for, boy?'

Roland was already troubled by the events he'd been through, but now things seemed to have taken on an even more sinister slant. He was wary of Hawkspur. He's out to do me harm, thought Roland. He would have to be extremely careful with this strange man.

After another glance back at the slab, he said, ' I don't know, sir.'

Hawkspur moved towards Roland. 'Don't you? Then you must think about it, mustn't you? And when you've decided you must come and tell me what it is, mn?' He chuckled and laid his arm on Roland's shoulders.

Roland's antennae were on high alert. He didn't like the faux camaraderie shown by Hawkspur. He was about to break away when Hawkspur did it for him.

'And let me show you something else,' said Hawkspur, as

he beckoned with crooked finger. He led Roland over to a cupboard. 'What was the name again?'

'Roland Anthony Wright, sir.'

He opened it and, to Roland's utter surprise, took out a besom – a witches broom.

'Well, Wright. *This* is a broom,' he said, pressing it onto him. '*This* is a bucket. *This* a dustpan. Mn?'

Roland took the dustpan in his hand, bewildered by Hawkspur's actions.

Hawkspur guided him to a pile of broken glass and smashed wood. '*This* was a previous experiment. You perceive a possible causal connection?' He waited for Roland's reply.

'Clean it up, sir?'

Hawkspur smiled in gratified reply. 'I shall be in my study,' he said, and strode off.

Roland started to clean up the mess, then thought of another thing to ask the fast-disappearing Hawkspur. 'Sir?'

But Hawkspur had reached his study and closed the door just before Roland spoke.

Roland applied himself to clearing up. As he worked, he glanced up at the plinth. He couldn't resist taking a closer look. He put the dustpan down on the control panel but, unfortunately, its weight pressed down one of the buttons. A huge spark leapt across the two spheres and Roland saw, in that brief moment, the outline of a human figure on the plinth.

Hawkspur's study was a small, book-lined room with a desk and a shaded lamp, an ornate orary, and a full-sized skeleton on a stand. The main object in the room was a sarcophagus on an old trolley. The hinged lid was closed.

There was a knock on the door and Roland called from outside. 'Sir? Doctor Hawkspur?'

Hawkspur got up from his chair and stood in a place where, if the door opened, he would be concealed from Roland's eyeline.

'Doctor Hawkspur,' Roland called out once more.

The door handle turned and Roland entered the study cautiously. He was immediately fascinated, despite himself, with the sarcophagus. He closed the door, still without seeing Hawkspur and moved towards it carefully...

Hawkspur made Roland jump when he spoke from behind him. 'And what pray, do you think you are doing? Mn?'

Roland turned to face him and said, 'Looking for you, sir. I was looking for you, sir.'

Hawkspur pulled a face. 'Were you?'

'Yes, sir.'

'And what conclusion have you reached?'

'About the machine?'

Hawkspur nodded.

Roland turned towards the sarcophagus. 'Is it... something to do with this, sir?'

'It is indeed, boy! Here we have the human form dormant and inert, and there...' He waved in the direction of the laboratory, 'we have the spark, the spark of intelligence. So. What might... come about, if I combined the two, mn?'

There was a pause as Roland figured out what was going on. 'You're going to create a human being?'

'Why not?'

Roland began to feel worried. He was unconvinced and scared.

'The challenge,' Hawkspur continued. 'The challenge...' He started to push the sarcophagus and its trolley and urged Roland, 'Come on boy, heave!'

Together, Hawkspur and Roland pushed the squeaking trolley, with the sarcophagus on top of it, out of the room, and wheeled it gingerly to the plinth.

The effort of the push exhausted Hawkspur but he was in his element – in the grip of his vision. He got his breath before stating, 'Man has always striven for perfection; I shall attain it! The body wears out before the mind, boy. It is weak, fallible, prey to accident and decay... There is never enough time, and far too much to learn! But this, my construct...' Hawkspur twisted the trolley towards the left of a bench. 'Left, left a touch.'

They manoeuvred the trolley around the bench.

Hawkspur continued his soliloquy. 'My construct will be impervious, indestructible! I shall teach him everything. He will know all there is to know... and when the experiment is complete, I shall have manufactured a genius!' He stopped pushing to savour the thought.

'And what will you do with him?' asked Roland quietly.

'He shall be my servant.' Hawkspur softened a little and smiled at Roland. 'There will be no further need of you. You can be on your way.'

They started pushing again.

'And you, sir?' enquired Roland.

'I shall stay here. Where else is there to go?'

'Out, sir? Outside?'

Hawkspur shook his head in a moment of sadness. 'I have

been here too long. Besides, this is my life's work, my world. What else could I need?'

Roland felt it was time to ask. 'Sir, could you show me where the key is?'

They gave one more heave and arrived at the plinth.

Hawkspur smiled ambiguously. 'First, let me show you...' He slowly raised the sarcophagus lid.

Roland looked in and gasped when he saw what was inside.

'My creation...' yelled Hawkspur manically, with immense pride, 'Ergon!'

Roland was horrified when he saw the sad sight of the figure in the sarcophagus. More like a monster than a creation, he thought. As he looked closer, he began to realise that Ergon bore a fairly strong resemblance to Mr Hawker, his singing teacher, but with a white face. His wild mop of black hair was similar to Vein's, but with one terrible difference – the hair had been very roughly stitched on to his head, and the stitches showed! The pathetic-looking creature was wearing crude, black woollen clothing, with an oversized jacket and clumping over-large boots, but sleeves and trousers that were too short. His hands were as white as his face, quite bloodless in appearance and manacled. It was weird. But everything Roland had experienced since the lift dropped had been weird, crazy and impossible.

Hawkspur was fiddling with his controls, monitoring them, making tiny adjustments. A loud thunderclap sounded as a charged spark flew between the spheres, then more sparks, as the noises started speeding up to a climax.

Hawkspur moved to a large square cage which had previously been hidden behind one of the benches. He called to Roland, 'Do you mind? If we could move this a bit nearer?'

Roland went to help him. They placed the cage next to the plinth.

'The beginnings of life are always traumatic,' said Hawkspur. He moved to a position close to the plinth and took charge of the controls. He looked down upon Ergon. 'Ergon! Ergon, live!' He turned up the power a touch more. 'Ergon, can you hear?'

No response came from the creature.

Hawkspur turned the controls up some more.

'Can I go now? Please? I want to go – I don't want to see any more,' pleaded Roland.

'You must always face the unknown,' said Hawkspur. 'Remember that! There is nothing to fear but life itself.'

Ergon began to twitch. The eyes opened first and the head began switching about, followed by the limbs jerking under electrical shock.

Hawkspur looked down at his wonderful creation with sheer delight. 'Success! You see?'

He quickly helped Ergon out of his sarcophagus and locked him firmly in the cage.

Ergon was more scared than angry as he shook the cage.

Hawkspur moved up to him and clicked his fingers.

Ergon stopped shaking the cage and stared blankly at Hawkspur's fingers.

'Good,' sighed Hawkspur. He moved in front of Roland to the other side of the cage, then clicked his fingers again.

Ergon turned his head towards the sound.

'Excellent hearing, perfect. Now – vision.' He moved slowly around so as not to alarm Ergon, and faced him in the cage. 'Ergon. I want you to listen to me. No one is going to harm you. You understand?' purred Hawkspur.

Roland watched incredulously as Hawkspur raised his index finger to the centre of Ergon's face, then moved it first to one side, then the other.

Ergon's eyes followed the movement without turning his head.

Hawkspur stood up, very proud of himself – the master of all he surveyed. He turned to Ergon. 'I am your master. You must do everything I say, do you understand? Nod your head if you do.' He made an exaggerated nod as an example to Ergon. 'Can you do that for me, Ergon? Now nod your head if you understand. Mn?'

Ergon moved his head slowly, stiffly, unaccustomed to the movement. He was watched eagerly by his master.

Roland was very wary of the monster. He kept well back from the cage, as if anticipating an attack through the bars, as the master continued to train his servant.

'Good. Now turn around. Turn around to your right.'

Ergon paused, obviously thinking about the move he had to make. It was as if he was unwilling to leave the sight of his master.

Hawkspur was elated. 'Now look at my assistant, Ergon.'

Roland and Ergon's eyes met for the first time. Roland felt both revulsion and pity for the monster slave.

'He will not harm you. Now, walk towards the boy.'

With awkward, stiff movements, Ergon shuffled across the cage to face Roland.

Hawkspur's eyes glittered with excitement as he proceeded with the training exercises. 'Now I want you to bow. Watch Roland and he will show you. Bow, Roland! Show him.'

Roland didn't like the idea, but felt it wiser to go along with Hawkspur – at least until he could discover a way out, and escape him and his horrible construct creature. Roland was now even more convinced that it bore an incredible similarity to Hawker, his teacher in... another world. One that he had stumbled out of and wished, oh so much, to get back to. Suddenly, Roland saw Hawkspur glaring at him.

'Show him... if you would be so kind,' said Hawkspur, slightly irritated by Roland's slow reaction to his orders.

Roland bowed to Ergon, but the creature's eyes swung back to those of its master.

Hawkspur was angered by this, and it showed when he said with raised voice, 'Look at Roland, will you?'

Totally cowed by his master's abrasive tone, Ergon obediently turned back to face Roland.

'Now, Ergon. Bow to him.'

Ergon slowly bowed to Roland.

'Good. Come here Ergon.'

The creature returned to face Hawkspur and awaited further instructions.

'Kneel. Down on your knees. Kneel to me. I am your master.'

Ergon looked at his master with puppy-like devotion.

'Now say: Master.' Hawkspur waited but nothing came from Ergon's mouth. Hawkspur repeated his order and made exaggerated mouth movements to help him. 'Come on. Maaaaster. Ma-sssss-ter. Go on, say it!'

Ergon still didn't respond.

'Your mouth, Ergon! Speak!'

In response Ergon made the appropriate mouth movements, but no sound came from it.

'Master! Repeat after me: Master! I order you to speak.'

Roland began to feel real pity for Ergon. He watched as Hawkspur became more and more heated.

'Speak to me, Ergon!' Hawkspur shouted.

Roland watched in amazement as he saw Ergon's eyes fill with tears. The monster contorted his face, trying to get the word out. The contortion began to affect his whole body as he shook in his effort to muster up a voice.

Hawkspur stared at him with total disbelief, then cried, 'Oh no!' He turned to Roland, in utter despair. 'A perfect specimen in every way but this. Everything but a voice.' He turned back to the cage where Ergon was cringing on the floor at his master's wrath. Hawkspur spoke to Roland in a lowered voice, 'I will have to start again...'

But Ergon had heard the remark. He was terrified.

'You can't,' said Roland, not really sure if he meant it.

Hawkspur rubbed his hands together and now sounded businesslike and determined. 'I must. He must be perfect!'

'But he's alive now. You can't just destroy a life because of your mistake,' said Roland, aware he was the only advocate for poor Ergon.

'Why not? Mn? I created him, I can destroy him. Do you know what a construct is boy? Mn? It is a machine.'

The words seemed to hold some kind of memory for Roland, of something in the past, but he battled on with his argument – and felt he could be a little more demanding. 'It is not,' he said, standing his ground.

Hawkspur overrode him. 'A machine through which the will of its creator can emerge. And when that machine does not work then it must be scrapped! Jettisoned! Abandoned!'

Roland looked down at Ergon, cringing on the floor of the cage. 'Can't you give him a voice?'

Hawkspur hardly heard him and chuntered on regardless, 'The waste! So perfect, so docile.' He interrupted himself. 'What did you say?'

Roland was pleased that he'd been listened to at last. 'Can't you improvise? Give him a voice of some kind?'

Hawkspur became thoughtful. He looked at Roland and then at the scrabbling Ergon... then back at Roland.

Roland felt a thinnest veil of success come over him as he saw Hawkspur warm to his idea.

'Give him a voice? Why not?' continued Hawkspur. 'You stay here. Calm him, pacify him,' he said as he hurried off.

'How?' called Roland.

'You said you could sing, didn't you? Sing to him,' came Hawkspur's odd reply.

Roland mulled this over. He couldn't recall having mentioned singing at all, since he'd arrived in this crazy new topsy-turvy world... It would be the thing furthest from his mind, he thought.

Ergon caught his attention. He was dashing from side to side in the cage.

Roland moved closer and tried to soothe him. 'Ergon, no. Please listen Ergon... It'll be all right. Don't worry. Ssh.' It had no effect, so he decided he might as well try singing.

Roland sang the first line of the solo piece he'd done so badly at his school. This time it went perfectly, not a note out of place, and he was relieved to see the monster calm down – first seeming puzzled, then smiling.

As Roland finished his song, Hawkspur emerged from his study, carrying a strange-looking contraption which was a bit like the bell of a trumpet with a mute stuck into it. What concerned Roland most was that it also had a leather headstrap fixed to it.

Hawkspur went up to the cage with his strange horn and noted that Ergon had tears in his eyes. 'Tears? It'll all be better soon. Here.' He proffered the strap and mute to Ergon, who cowered away from it. 'Here is a voice for you, Ergon.' He made an aside to Roland. 'From a previous experiment.' He turned back to Ergon and began to try and win his confidence. 'Ergon. A voice... to help you speak.' He stuck the bell and mute into Ergon's mouth. 'Turn around now.'

The construct obediently turned around and Hawkspur fastened the strap around his neck.

Poor Ergon looked a sad sight, thought Roland, as he continued to look on at the proceedings. He had no idea what Hawkspur was going to do, but he was starting to feel that it might be something not very nice.

'There we are. Turn around Ergon.'

He did so...

'You have a voice now. Your master has given you a voice. Your maaa-sssss-ter.'

Ergon tried to say the word, but it came out slurring uncontrollably up and down the tonal scale, an awful hideous noise. 'Maaaaaaaaaaaaaasssssssssstttteeerrrrrrrr...'

A glass vessel on a bench smashed under the impact of the vibrating sound waves.

Even Ergon was horrified by the noise coming out of him!

Hawkspur, fearful for his experiments, ordered Ergon to desist. 'Quiet, Ergon. Quiet!'

Ergon subsided, then slumped down inside his cage, muttering and growling, relapsing into subhuman gutturals.

Hawkspur whispered to Roland, 'It's no use, he will have to be destroyed.' He looked at Ergon sadly. 'Oh Ergon, what did I do wrong?'

Roland hesitated, then went on with his observation. 'Perhaps you shouldn't have made a...' He faltered, as Hawkspur's eyes narrowed.

'Made a what?'

Roland worried. On one hand, he should just shut up and worry about getting out of the nightmare he'd found himself in. On the other, he felt he should say how he felt about what was going on. He muttered, 'Perhaps you shouldn't have set out to make a slave.' There. He'd said it. He mentally prepared himself for Hawkspur's retort.

'And why not, pray?'

'You could have made him your equal.'

'What?' shouted Hawkspur. 'Equal?' The very idea was anathema to him. 'No. This was the only way.' Hawkspur gave Roland a worrying, calculating look again. 'Unless, of course, we can find a real voice, boy. Mn?' He grabbed Roland by the shoulder and held him close.

Roland was looking directly into his glittering demonic eyes.

'I need *your* voice.' In a speedy action, Hawkspur, with his superior strength, dragged Roland to the plinth and quickly manacled first one hand and then the other.

Roland tried to resist but, perhaps because of the pecking order he was so aware of, he didn't resist quite enough and found himself laid out on the plinth, strapped down and unable to move. His mind began to race. Surely Hawkspur didn't mean it, he thought. How could he possibly take my voice? But as he pushed against the straps on his arms and legs, he began to feel rather depressed at the way things were turning out...

Ergon was sitting on a swivel chair next to the plinth. The mute contraption had been taken off. He had a sullen look on his face.

Hawkspur was busy connecting a couple of electrodes. One passed through copper tubing to the vocal chord area on Roland's neck. The other went to the speech area of Ergon's brain. When satisfied, and after a final tweak on his controls, Hawkspur smiled grimly at Roland. 'You see, in the end, boy, there is no one you should really trust here.' He moved to a timer and made a minute adjustment. 'I *must* take your voice...' He threw a lever and the spark crackled and shot between the spheres as his voice became strident, '... to teach my child to sing!'

'I won't let you, I won't let you!' cried Roland, tugging at his restraints.

'It is useless to resist,' said Hawkspur in a benign, almost sorry tone.

Roland turned his howls of protest into a chant. 'I won't, I won't, I won't, I won't!'

Hawkspur shouted above it. 'You will stay here until you do!'

'I won't, I won't, I won't!' chanted Roland.

'We shall see, when I return.' With that, Hawkspur moved away.

Roland continued his chanting, 'I won't, I won't, I won't!' But slowly it began to happen...

At first, Ergon's mouth was miming Roland's chant, then his voice chimed in and gained in strength as Roland's began to fade.

'I won't, I won't, I won't!' chanted Roland.

But Ergon took over the chant. 'I won't – I won't – I won't – I won't – I won't!'

Roland suddenly realised that his voice was disappearing. He was no longer chanting, just mouthing the words.

Ergon was delighted with his 'I wont's'. He grinned at Roland and tried to encourage him with some signs to say more words.

Roland decided to keep his mouth tight shut, and shook his head firmly.

In a place in another world, Sergeant Tarr was leaning over, looking into the lift shaft. 'Son! Shout if you can hear me!'

He listened... Silence. Beside him were PC Briggs, Vine and Ripper. They too were listening.

There was a sound of footsteps, and Curry the engineer came into view. He was all oily and dirty – and angry. 'What the 'ell's goin' on, eh?' he said. 'I just had a switch panel blow out in me face!'

Back in Roland's world, a huge flash came from one sphere to another. It started up several more irregular flashes.

Roland craned his head around as far as he could and caught sight of the key to the cage, lying on a bench within Ergon's reach... A large gold key.

Roland wondered how he might get it. He got the creature's attention, saying, 'Ergon.'

Ergon repeated, 'Ergon,' and immediately took over the word, leaving Roland mouthing again. He grinned and pointed to himself. 'Ergon. Ergon,' he said.

Roland drew his attention to the key.

It took a while, but Ergon got the message and reached out for it.

Now comes the difficult bit, thought Roland. He mimed that Ergon should give him the key.

Ergon shook his head. 'I won't! Ergon.'

Roland nodded at him.

Again Ergon refused. 'I won't! Ergon.' He pointed to Roland's mouth, miming that if he would speak, Ergon would give him the key.

Roland nodded. He hoped that Ergon would understand that he wanted the key first.

Ergon refused at first, then gave in and handed Roland the key. 'I won't,' said Ergon.

Now Roland was faced with the task of shorting out the machine with only his wrist free. He was aiming to flick the key into the path of the sparks...

He carefully measured with his eye.

Ergon became impatient and encouraged him to speak. 'Ergon! Ergon! Ergon!

Roland decided it was now or never, and tossed the key

into the path of the electrical transmissions. The key was caught in the lightning flash and vibrated and spun, held there by the power. There was a huge bang and all the circuitry started to short out and blow. Smoke, crackles and sizzles came from the machine.

Roland began to wonder what, exactly, he had achieved, but he was desperate. He just had to get free. He pulled and pulled at his wrist restraints and finally freed one arm and then the next, then wrenched the electrodes from his neck.

It was then that he heard a huge scream of anguish from Ergon. 'I won't...'

Roland gave him a sympathetic look and said, 'Sorry, Ergon.' He pulled his legs free.

Ergon just sat himself down, staring uncomprehendingly at Roland's efforts.

Roland ran for it and headed for the same stairs he'd come in by.

Hawkpsur reappeared and quickly appreciated what was happening. He opened the cage and yelled at Ergon, 'Ergon, after him!'

Ergon vehemently replied, 'I won't!'

'Ergon you must! He's taking your voice.'

Ergon put all his strength into the only reply he could make, 'I won't!' – but he meant the opposite. He lumbered off after Roland, who was galloping up the stairs.

Roland tripped and fell forward, then howled in pain. It was a nightmare moment. But when he saw Ergon approaching, he forgot his fall and started to scramble up the stairs again.

Ergon was close enough to grab at Roland's ankles. He

missed them and in his frustration let out hideous, animal-like noise.

Now Hawkspur, too, was chasing up the stairs.

Roland reached the circular gallery. There were doors all around and he tried one, then another, but found himself in another nightmare scenario – all the doors were locked. Even worse, there were no handles on them.

Ergon and Hawkspur reached the gallery and Hawkspur pointed out a direction. 'That way, Ergon.'

Ergon moved one way while Hawkspur went the other. They had Roland trapped.

In desperation, Roland tried another door. It opened outwards and he could see nothing beyond, but in his panic Roland stepped into the darkness... and fell into black, Stygian depths.

'After him!' shouted Hawkspur.

Ergon dashed after him.

Roland found himself back in the corridor with the stone heads. They appeared to turn as Roland passed them, and the arms flailed and tried to grasp at him, impeding his progress.

Meanwhile, the lumbering Ergon was closing on him, roaring away in the background, 'I wont! I won't!'

Roland rounded a corner, fending off one of the arms, and saw a flight of stone steps winding up towards a dim light. He glanced back at Ergon, now dangerously close, then dashed up the steps and round a bend in the stairway... only to come face to face with an outlandish figure, who towered above Roland and was outlined in the light behind him. He was dressed in strange armour: half Samurai, half fantasy, in the style of a heavy metal album cover.

Roland was frozen to the spot. As he saw the face of the Warrior more clearly, he was able to see that this person bore a passing resemblance to Ripper.

The Warrior gave a Samurai double-handed challenge, presenting his sword blade at his adversary. Roland could tell he was very tensed up. The challenger then yelled his battle cry, 'Haghhhhhha!'

Roland stepped back from the vicious looking blade, then saw that Ergon had caught up...

Roland was trapped.

Chapter Three

The knights who to the Dark Tower's search addressed
Their steps – that just to fail as they, seemed best,
And all the doubt was now – should I be fit?

ROLAND'S MIND was in a whirl as the Warrior blurted out staccato, almost Japanese-sounding, challenges, with a strange English accent that were more like a dog bark than normal speech.

'Wouldya! Ah! Wouldya! Ah! Staircase is a Warrior's. You are on a Warrior's stairs. Fight! Yah!' The Warrior made a sudden swish of his sword – which was a bit too close for comfort – then struck another martial attitude.

Roland flattened himself against the wall as the wailing Ergon arrived yelling, 'I won't!'

Both Roland's adversaries leaped on him, but he was small and nimble enough to dodge out of their way, making them collide with each other. They both fell to the floor, as Roland got a few steps above them, then paused briefly to see the outcome.

Ergon got up, bemused at having missed Roland. He became angrier than ever. He ripped a small, round-studded shield from the wall and armed himself with a firebrand, which he took from its holder.

The Warrior was hopping mad to have been humiliated by his quarry. He took an attack pose. And then the fight was on in earnest, with slash and clank of weapons.

Relieved to see they were more interested in fighting each other than him, Roland took the opportunity to dart away up the steps, putting a reasonably safe distance between him and his enemies. He looked back to see Ergon and the Warrior going at it hammer and tongs, shouting their respective whoops of battle. He sort of admired the Warrior – he obviously had style – but the lumbering Ergon had brute strength and endurance and, it seemed, an indifference to pain.

Against his will, Roland became mesmerised by the fight going on below him. He kept watching as Ergon smashed the pitch brand down on the Warrior's shoulder armour.

Swish! The Warrior's sword whipped through the air in front of Ergon's face, only to end up cutting into a thin carved pillar.

Ergon's next wild swing hit the pillar next to it.

To Roland, the sounds of the fight began to merge into a kind of comic-book style, as the two fighters swung at each other to and fro across the landing. Instead of *Clang! Slash! Bang!* the sounds seemed to become *Splatt! Thwock! Claaaaang! Yaaargh!*

Roland was sure that Ergon was getting the upper hand, but the Warrior continued to attack, attack, attack – aggression to the last breath.

Then, an almighty swinging blow by Ergon made the Warrior step back smartly. He hit the pillar with a thump; the pillar cracked and looked very unstable.

Obviously Ergon thought he'd defeated the Warrior and he lunged forward in triumph. But, as he raised the pitch brand, ready for the *coup de grace*, he tripped on the uneven surface.

The Warrior quickly stepped aside.

Ergon could not stop and went charging into the slim pillars, which gave way as he clutched at them. Poor Ergon flew out into a seemingly bottomless well of black space, screaming as he and echoing as he fell, 'I wonnnnnnnnnnn't!'

Down and down.

'I wonnnnnnnnnnnnnnnnnnn't!'

Roland expected the Warrior to be triumphant at winning, but instead, he shouted down into the abyss, 'No! You can't! Come back and fight! You must fight! Warrior's stairs – you must fight! Fight me!' In his anger he began to fling his sword about, fighting and slashing at shadows.

Roland was puzzled. He frowned as he watched this crazy display of Bushido-Kendo, but he couldn't find an answer to the Warrior's behaviour.

It was during this pause that a hand clasped him by the scruff and abruptly jerked him into the darkness of the small landing on the stairs...

Roland couldn't see who his assailant was, but immediately thought what a fool he'd been not to keep running. He guessed that it was Hawkspur who held him by the neck. He panicked and wondered if he ought to apologise for the loss of his horrible creature... Then, he thought better of it, deciding to let events dictate his next move.

On the next floor down, the Warrior was still ranting. 'I want blood! Want flesh! Warrior without enemies is nothing! Nothing! Nothing! Nothing! No... No...' Then he seemed frightened and looked up at something, or someone, Roland couldn't see. 'No... No... Let me live! Let me fight! Let me live!'

To Roland's surprise, the Warrior slowly faded away. He felt a tug from the person who was holding him. It pushed him, guiding him, as a voice said, 'Come on you, hurry.'

The voice told Roland that it was Vein who had hold of him, and he relaxed a little. 'Why?' he asked. 'Will he come after us?'

'No,' said Vein. 'He'll be waiting for us.'

'Where?' asked Roland, now getting a bit wary of Vein.

'On the staircase, where else?'

'But we've just left him,' said Roland, puzzled.

Vein let go of Roland and faced him. 'The Warrior is always on the stairs. That's what he's there for. To stop people like you. And you're not ready for him yet...'

They started walking, Vein leading.

'When will I be ready?' asked Roland, quite concerned.

'How should I know?' said Vein irritably. 'I can't help it! I got nothin' to do with the staircase. Not my job.'

Roland mulled this over and then said, 'What is your job then, Mr Vein?'

He gave Roland a sour glance. 'For the moment *you* are. I been detailed.'

'Who by?' Roland played a hunch. '*Them*?'

Vein became suspicious and looked sideways at him. 'How did you know about *them*?'

Roland opened up with his theory of everything, 'Well, I learned quite a bit from Hawkspur. That's what I'm here for, isn't it? To learn things?'

Vein looked at him but said nothing, just turned and went off down the corridor.

Roland followed in his wake. He felt it was worth another go at Vein, in the hope of getting a response. 'He told me not to trust *you* for a start.'

A sly grin from Vein. 'And did you trust Doctor Hawkspur?'

'He told me to trust no one.'

'You haven't got any choice have you?'

'Yes,' said Roland in a spirited way. 'That's something else I've learned.'

Vein stopped dead in his tracks. 'And what might that be?' he said, very seriously.

'I don't need you. Or your stupid keys.'

'Don't you?' said Vein quietly.

'No, I don't. I can go straight up. Up to the top and out.'

'Go on then,' said Vein.

'I'm going.' He gave Vein a curt nod as he marched off. 'Farewell'.

But Vein was grinning as he watched him go off.

Roland reached a curve in the corridor and another flight of steps going up. He started up it, full of hope and confidence, but when he reached the first bend he found that it was blocked off. There was nothing there but a blank stone wall.

He searched around the wall. Maybe, he thought, there was a special opening, a secret door. Anything was possible in this crazy world. But, search as he may, he couldn't find a way of getting through. Frustrated he called out in anger, 'Vein!'

He heard Vein's laughter rippling through the corridor below in reply.

Roland retraced his steps and walked back along the corridor, to where he'd left him, but when he reached the spot, there was nobody there.

Roland felt a cold fear, mixed with frustration, rising and churning inside him. He went a little further, but was terrified that he would meet the Warrior – or Hawkspur – again, and be back where he'd started.

He turned around yet again and there, just where he'd left Vein, he saw something lying on the ground. A key. A huge, bright red key.

What did it open? thought Roland. He slowly bent down and picked it up, intrigued by the strange, metallic red colour. It was like no other key he'd ever seen.

Then, beyond him, he suddenly noticed a door with a heart shaped keyhole...

In that other world, the parallel universe Roland was striving to get back to, in the apartment where he used to live...

The Wright's living room was lit by a red-shaded lamp,

which was glowing in the corner. The red curtains had been drawn, giving the room a look of a warm summer sunset. The stereo was quietly playing the kind of soft, middle of the road music that June enjoyed and Ron abhorred – though he never said so. This one was her favourite, the Nelson Riddle Orchestra playing hit tunes from the shows.

June was at the table, laying out clock patience around the glass bowl centrepiece. She had tidied up since Ron had left and taken away all his clutter. The living room looked warm and feminine.

She responded to a knock at the door, 'All right, Roland, love, come in. It's not locked.'

The door opened and a stranger's voice called out, 'Mrs Wright? Police here.'

June's reaction was to push all the cards into a heap as she stood up, a bit flustered. 'What?' she frowned.

'Can I come in?' said Sergeant Tarr – having already entered.

'Yes, of course. Come in.'

Sergeant Tarr nodded and presented her with a troubled look. 'Good evening, Mrs Wright. Er... Sergeant Tarr, Southmead Station.

'Yes? Whatever is it?'

'Roland Wright. Your son, is he?'

'Stepson, yes. Nothing's happened has it?'

'Well, we hope not. We think he's got stuck in the lift.'

She had a flash of intuition. 'Not that lot on the stairs again, was it?'

'There was... a bit of a set-to.'

'I knew it.' She shook her head. 'They're all yobbos, every one of them.'

'Yes,' said Sergeant Tarr calmly. 'He ran into the lift and down it went. We've been shouting, but there's no reply. Only, would you like to have a try, Mrs Wright? He might be a bit scared of us, like.'

She was already moving to the door as she answered, her voice full of concern. 'Yes, of course. Oh lord, I hope he's all right.'

Roland looked down at the red key, then up at the heart-shaped lock. He carefully inserted the key into the keyhole and turned it. The lock clicked, he pushed the door open and went in.

He came upon a similar pattern of architecture to the place he had just left: a circular gallery with a flight of stairs leading down to the main area. But these stairs were sparkling white and had a blood-red carpet on them...

He tiptoed down the stairs into the room below which, despite being much bigger, bore a certain similarity to the living room of Flat 1605. The floor had the same cushion-floor design, but with a much enlarged pattern. The heap of cushions were all red and arranged like an Eastern divan. Another difference was that the furniture was covered in a red material, like dust-covers, but shiny. The only uncovered item was the white table. On it – instead of a glass with falling snow – sat a crystal ball with a pack of Tarot cards beside it.

Roland could smell a rather pleasant perfume hanging

in the air. It reminded him of something... he couldn't remember what.

Roland descended the stairs to the room below. When he got to the room, he noted that the sideboard was the same as the one in his flat.

A door clicked open and then closed. Roland was surprised to see a lady, who looked uncannily like his stepmother, coming towards him in greeting with open arms. Roland's image of her was that of June, but not June. She was theatrically made up and wore a low-cut, long, extravagant gown.

'Welcome my child, welcome!' The Lady put her arms around Roland in an effusive, smothering welcome.

It was with the kind of intimacy that Roland would normally have shunned. He was still on his guard after his last encounter, but as she touched him, he felt a strangely warm glow and allowed himself to be embraced. To Roland her manner seemed warm – and yet false.

The Lady smiled at him and said, 'Let me greet you. Oh, my poor boy, what have they done to you?'

Roland stood his ground and endured her embrace, then disengaged himself. With the briefest of smiles, he said, 'I'm all right.' He was still confused by the warmth of her greeting. And then there was the perfume, a sort of clinging odour, that made him feel something between pleasantness and revulsion. Roland muttered, 'But I'm supposed to...' His memory went blank for a second.

'Supposed to what, my precious?'

Roland gathered his scrambled thoughts together and told her, 'Supposed to be... finding my way out.'

'Oh, my poor one, no. You must stay. Come, sit down.'

She sat Roland down on the cushions.

He wondered if he should be sitting there, but events seemed to be overtaking him at that moment.

The Lady sat down next to him. 'You must forget. Forget your distress, you are here now... It is over,' she said, with a self-satisfied smile, and began to smooth his hair.

This, Roland objected to, but experienced the polarisation again – his feelings were caught between pleasure and irritation. He could think of no good reason to stop her.

'You must be hungry? Yes? Thirsty after your ordeal? See, I have prepared things for you, food and drink.' She clapped her hands, but nothing happened. There was a pause, then, 'Vein! Vein! Where are you?' she shouted irritably. She turned to Roland and said, 'Forgive me, please, my boy.'

Vein appeared from behind the red silk wall hangings. 'Yes, m'lady?'

'Serve us, you ugly creature!' snapped the Lady.

Vein's reply was flat and rather bored. 'Yes, m'lady.'

He then disappeared behind the wall hanging from whence he'd come.

The Lady smiled at Roland warmly. 'Why so tense? You must relax. You are safe here, you are home. Listen...' She waved her hand and soft, tinkling music started to play.

It sounded rather like the Asian prayer wheels Roland had once seen on a television programme, all soothing and lulling. He listened for a while, then built up the courage to blurt out, 'You're very kind, but this isn't my home.'

The Lady said in feigned shock, 'Is it not better, my poor, thin boy? I shall look after you, care for you, give you everything you want!'

Vein came in again, trundling an ornate trolley of goodies.

Roland could see fruit and strange-shaped bottles of drink, but their colours were too bright, too unreal and the fruit was waxy and overlarge, green, purple and acid yellow...

Roland again tried to take a stand, 'But I want to get out of here.'

Vein sniggered at this.

The Lady yelled at Vein, 'Out!'

'I shall, m'lady,' murmured Vein as he turned sharply and made his way out.

Roland appealed to the Lady, 'Will you help me, please?'

'But of course my child... If that is your wish. But first, refresh yourself. Take what you like.'

The Lady pushed the trolley nearer to him.

Roland was intrigued by the bright colours of the fruit and the rainbow-coloured drinks, but there was something in the back of his mind that cautioned him not to drink. He felt that such garish coloured beverages were somehow 'not nice' – he hesitated to think they might be poisonous or contain some drug or other.

His misgivings were enough to make him refuse – as politely as possible. 'No, thank you very much.' To break the moment, he picked up the crystal ball. He turned to her, holding it up to the light. 'What is this?'

'Don't you know? It's crystal.'

He continued. 'And these cards and things?' He pointed out the Tarot cards.

'They help me in my pursuits,' the Lady said, after considering her answer.

Roland was not satisfied and pressed on. 'What pursuits?'

She answered this with an enigmatic smile.

'Are you a fortune teller or something?' asked Roland.

'Seer. I'm a seer.'

Roland had no idea what this meant. 'Oh,' he said making his answer equivocal.

'I look into the future and the past,' she said, as she moved to the other side of the crystal ball and sat down. 'Shall I show you?'

At this point, Roland began to feel a uncomfortable. This kind of thing was creepy, and well out of his comfort zone. 'Mumbo-jumbo' was what he called anything even slightly supernatural.

'Would you like to see what lies in wait for you?'

He was unsure if he did or not want to know. 'Will it be the truth?'

'The future cannot be altered. Look.' She held the crystal between her hands. It filled with white smoke, which then dispersed slowly. 'See, the mist clears...'

Roland moved closer and looked into the crystal ball. He couldn't be sure if what he then saw was real, or if it was something that was coming from his own befuddled mind. There seemed to be swirling hypnotic patterns... As he stared at the livid colours, he became mesmerised by it.

Then came her voice, lifting him out of his trance. 'Roland. Roland, did you see?'

He still felt a bit woozy, and answered in a flat, monotonous voice. 'Yes... yes... I did...'

The Lady smiled and said, 'Outside here, there is nothing.'

He found himself repeating what she said, 'Nothing.'

'Only emptiness and confusion, forever.'

'Forever,' repeated Roland. He felt himself losing control

of his body. It was something he could not fight and he gave way at the knees and slumped down on the table.

The Lady quickly supported him and held him in her arms. Her face was close to his. That perfume smell, the paint and powder of her heavy make-up...

She looked him directly in the eye and said in an encouraging voice, 'This is where you should be, Roland, you understand?'

Roland nodded, but was barely aware of what was happening to him. He had an overwhelming desire to get out – get away from the state in which he found himself – but it was as if the his brain's instructions weren't getting through to his bone, muscle and nerves.

The Lady purred on, 'You have reached your goal. This is where you must stay. Here, here with me.'

Again, Roland found himself nodding at the Lady.

She smiled to herself, in total victory. 'Come, rest now, my wounded soldier...'

She helped him over to the pile of red cushions and allowed him to collapse into them. She stood over him and he heard her echoing, soothing, voice in his head, 'When you awake, we will eat of the fruit of eternal youth and drink of the wine of forgetfulness... and then my child, we shall have peace and warmth and each other. There will be no future and no past for you Roland, my child...' Her voice speeded up, and became more urgent. 'Never grow up, never grow away, never turn against me, never leave me. I shall have your heart for ever...'

Roland was trying to shake his head, open his eyes, and move his lips to challenge her, but try as he might, he couldn't move a muscle.

She looked down at him with a loving smile. 'Oh Roland, how happy we shall be.'

Roland let this thought stay unanswered for the moment. That's it, thought Roland, keep mum... then realised what an unfortunate turn of phrase he'd used.

In a parallel world, elsewhere...

June and Sergeant Tarr walked up to the knot of people standing around the lift entrance. There were the two engineers, Vine, PC Briggs – who was still holding on to Ripper, and a few gongoozlers from that floor of the building.

PC Briggs held them well away from the lift.

Vine gave June a weak grin. 'Oh hello, Mrs Wright. Terrible business, isn't it?'

Sergeant Tarr led June past Vine to the lift, to the open yawning doors.

She hesitated, not wishing to get closer. She actively tried to pull back from the brink.

Sergeant Tarr held on to her, then leaned her forward so she could see right down over the precipitous edge of the lift shaft. 'Okay, Mrs Wright. I've got you,' he said.

June was really worried, but steeled herself to look down. 'Roland! Roland, love – you all right?'

There was silence as they all waited for some sort of reply, then June looked at Sergeant Tarr, very upset, tears welling up.

He nodded at the lift shaft, encouraging her to try once more. 'And again. Try again.'

'Roland! Roland!' she shouted at the top of her voice.

They waited but there was still no response.

She pulled herself back, overcome by emotion. 'I can't,' she said firmly. I can't...'

Sergeant Tarr understood what she must be going through and drew her back from the edge.

She turned to one of the engineers. 'Can't you go down and get him out?' she pleaded.

'Not as simple as that, love. We've had to turn the power off. All the other doors are jammed shut, and this 'un's jammed open...'

Sergeant Tarr interrupted. 'Try once again Mrs Wright, can you? You never know.'

June thought it over and decided she ought to try once more, for poor Roland's sake. Sergeant Tarr held her tight by the arm and she looked down into the dark chasm again.

'Roland! Ro... land!'

She heard nothing and saw nothing but the frightening dark abyss of the shaft...

The Lady called out to the sleeping Roland, curled up on the cushions. 'Roland?' She bent over him, smiling, and kissed his forehead. 'Wake, my child.'

Roland's eyes opened slowly and he smiled happily, dreamily...

Then he looked up at her.

'You fell asleep,' she said.

Roland sat up and looked around, feeling strangely delighted to be where he was. He caught hold of the Lady's hand and smiled up at her. He shifted to lean on his elbow. He couldn't remember ever feeling so relaxed and pleasant... Then he frowned. 'You know, there are dark things. Things in the past.'

The Lady suddenly looked hesitant, worried.

'But I can't honestly remember.'

The Lady looked relieved and smiled down at him.

'I don't want to remember, do I?' he said, quite brightly.

She poured him a drink of a thick, bright orange, liquid. 'Of course not.'

'I am at home here. Safe, warm, at peace.'

She proffered the drink and an oversized, very, very, bright red apple. 'Then would you like to stay here... forever?'

'Oh yes,' said Roland taking the drink.

She looked pleased and happy at his acceptance of the situation. 'Eat, drink, my little one.'

He took the glass and was about to sink his teeth into what appeared to be a most succulent fruit, when Vein entered in a hurry. 'Excuse me, my Lady,' he said, and hurried towards Roland who was about to take a bite out of the apple.

She screamed at Vein. 'Get out!'

Roland was shocked by the Lady's angry, vitriolic tone.

'Yes, m'lady,' came Vein's answer, and he backed slowly out of the room and slammed the door shut.

Roland bit into the apple and said, as he chewed, 'Who was that ugly creature?'

'A servant. He has his uses. Come, drink!' She held up a

glass of yellow liquid, clinking her glass against his as she toasted Roland. 'To our happiness and forgetfulness.'

They drank together.

In the room, behind the red curtains...

Vein had not gone out, but just slammed the door from the inside. He watched them from the edge of the curtain, eating and drinking and smiling and lounging about.

'A Caliban's eye view,' he muttered softly to himself. 'She's got you now, hasn't she? Got you in her power. There's nothing I can do now. You're doomed, boy. Doomed to everlasting bliss.'

'Shall I cast the cards for us?' asked the Lady brightly, picking up the Tarot pack.

Roland frowned, puzzled by the words.

'The cards of fortune. They will tell us our future. Do you want to see?'

At that moment Roland put a hand to his head. He'd suddenly begun to feel dizzy.

'What is it, my pet?' asked the Lady.

'Nothing. It's gone now. Just a bit dizzy.' He looked at the dregs of the liquid in his glass and put it down. 'I felt myself falling through darkness. Falling...'

'Come by me,' she said and patted the cushions beside her.

He seated himself by her side.

She turned over the first card. It was The Hanged Man...

Roland grimaced at the sight of it.

'The cards know everything,' the Lady said and began to lay them out in a circle. 'The Wheel of Fortune.' She placed two cards in the middle. 'These, the cards of destiny.' She looked at him. 'Yours and mine... choose one.'

Vein, watching from the curtain, closed his eyes shut tight as Roland reached out for a card. He crossed his fingers.

Roland's hand strayed first to one face-down card, then the other. Finally he decided and picked one up and showed it to her.

'The Emperor!' she gasped.

'What does it mean?' asked Roland.

She smiled before saying, 'You are to be king. The card says you are to be king.' She was quite excited by the thought. 'And I shall be your...' She reached out for the other card, then blanched at the sight of the toppling Tower, La Maison Dieu, '... destruction. No! It cannot be!' She swept the cards from the table in anger. 'They lie! They lie!'

She backed away in horror, then turned and rushed towards her boudoir, yelling, 'No! No!' as she slammed the door behind her.

Roland rushed after her, but her red bedroom door was locked tight. 'What is it?' he called. 'What's the matter? Please! Don't cry. Don't leave me! Please listen to me!' He could hear her sobbing inside her room and hammered on the door once more. 'Please don't cry. I love you – please don't cry.'

Inside her room, the Lady was lying face down on her bed, heaving sobs and sighs.

She stopped and listened to Roland's voice from outside.

'Listen to me – please don't cry – I love you –'

At his protestation of love, she lifted her head and smiled, as if to say: *Got you, my boy...*

On the other side of the door, Roland was disconsolate and walked back to the table. He sat down to wait for her return.

Vein emerged from the curtain where he'd been hiding.

'What do you want?' asked Roland tersely.

'You want to get out, boy – while you've got the chance.'

'What? What are you talking about?'

''You're in a very poor position, boyo, only you don't realise it, do you? Lolling about here in luxurious circumstances, talkin' about love.'

Roland was beginning to get annoyed. 'Nonsense! I am to be king. Look.' He showed Vein the Emperor card.

Vein snatched it roughly and tore it up. 'Means nothing, boy. You've had it. She's after your heart,' he said, pointing at the Lady's bedroom door.

'Why? That's rubbish,' said Roland with little interest.

'To keep you here. You shouldn't have eaten that apple or drank that stuff.'

'Why not?' I'm quite happy here.' He was getting indignant now.

'Happy is not the point. You're not here for that. You're here to progress – not loll about.'

'Nonsense!' exclaimed Roland.

'Is it?' As he spoke, Vein saw the boudoir door start to open and lowered his voice. 'Look, there's a way out here somewhere boy, if you can find it.'

The Lady came out of her boudoir and saw Vein. 'You! Leave the child alone! Get yourself out.'

'Just going, m'lady.'

'Out!' she yelled.

Vein obeyed her command but muttered under his breath, 'My Lady of the Castle.'

She crossed Vein, shuffling his way out, and put her arm around Roland. 'My poor boy.'

But Roland was more concerned about her. 'Why were you crying?'

'It doesn't matter now.'

Roland indicated the cards. 'Was it these? The cards?'

'It doesn't matter,' she insisted. She held her arms open to him. 'Oh my baby...'

He went to her. She held him against her and stroked his hair, his head against her bosom. 'Listen to me, Roland, you trust me, don't you? Whatever happens to either of us, it's so that we can be together, forever, and there is always a price to pay for happiness...'

For Roland things became curiouser and curiouser. As he looked up at the Lady, she began to tower above him. He felt a sickening unease at what was happening, but was again mesmerised by her silken tones.

'I had to do it, Roland. You might have grown away from me. I had to make you eat and drink to make you mine... My baby, my precious love.'

At last, Roland took in what had happened to him. He was no more than two inches tall, standing on the table like a tiny statuette. His voice came out thin and high. 'Help me. Help! Please!'

The Lady picked up her crystal ball and placed it on top of him.

*

Roland was inside the crystal ball, shouting and screaming to be let out. Now he regretted not listening to Vein. What has this woman done to him? What had he done to deserve such a fate? Self pity, mixed with anger, flooded his mind, but battering his fists on the glass wall had no effect at all on his predicament.

He looked out through the glass at the Lady's face, distorted by the prism of the glass.

'Please understand,' she said, her voice loud and echoing. 'You are *my* baby now. I will care for you, look after you... We will always have each other now. And you shall have new friends, my poor lonely boy.'

Roland could do nothing more than shout again and again, 'Let me out! Let me out!'

The Lady got up really close to the crystal ball and purred, speaking in baby talk, 'And you will never grow old, no. Not never, never, ever.'

Roland could only whimper. He had exhausted himself shouting.

'Hush, my little one, hush. I'll go and prepare you a place. And I'll find something nice for you to wear.' A final smile, horribly distorted in the glass, and she went off towards her boudoir.

Roland tried to find something, some way to release himself. He was getting desperate to find a way out, a crack, a fault in the glass or something. Just something! But he could find nothing...

All hope gone, Roland sank down in his glass cage. He wanted to cry but he couldn't; something was stopping him from giving up all hope.

Crying could come later...

He saw a new distorted face at the glass. It was Vein, who'd popped out of hiding yet again.

'Help me, Vein!' shouted Roland.

Vein pressed his ear against the crystal ball to hear what Roland was saying.

'Get me out!' shouted Roland.

Vein looked in at him sympathetically, but shook his head gravely. 'I can't. No I can't, y'see boy. Against the rules, isn't it? I told you – you have to make your own way.'

'Vein, please!' pleaded Roland.

Vein reiterated. 'I can't.' But then he did something. He put a cushion on the floor next to the table. 'That's all I can do, boy, and I shouldn't be doing that, by rights.' With that, Vein scuttled off.

Roland called to him as he departed. 'Vein! What's she going to do to me? What's she going to do?'

But Vein had gone.

Roland had an idea. He rushed at the glass sides of the crystal ball. It moved just a bit. He did it again and it moved some more, towards where Vein had put the cushion...

In the boudoir, the place was a froth of pink lace. The Lady was sorting through a frilly basket of dolls' clothes. She finally came up with a little grey velvet jacket and pantaloons and put them down on the bed. She looked at them, pleased with her choice, then got up and went over to her mantel shelf. On it, in glass cases, was June's collection of china figurines...

The Lady made a space for Roland between two shepherdesses. 'There,' she said. 'I think you'll be happy there, my boy.'

She was interrupted by the sound of the crystal ball rolling across the floor in the lounge and then smashing and shattering...

The Lady came out of the boudoir, distraught, carrying the little outfit she'd picked out for Roland to wear. She tiptoed around the shattered crystal ball.

'Roland! What have you done? Oh my poor boy,' she cried, as she caught sight of him, scampering for cover behind a furniture drape.

Roland noted that her concern was turning to anger, as she realised he was trying to escape.

'Roland!' Her tone sharpened as she crept towards the draped furniture.

He could see her shadow coming towards him and took off to another hiding place.

'Roland? Where are you?' She changed her tactics again, cajoling. 'Roland, my little one. What is it?'

He could sense she was getting closer. He waited in fear of being discovered.

'Oh Roland, come on. I haven't got time for games now. I want to show you your new clothes, Roland. Can't you hear me? Your new friends are waiting.'

Roland noted that her last words were very loud – and that she must be near. He made another desperate run for it. He found the edge of another drape and crawled underneath.

The Lady's voice was now very loud and very near. 'Roland? Are you there, Roland?'

He knew she was pretty well upon him and made yet another bid to get away from her. This time he went over open floor and she caught sight of him.

Her voice was now hardened, 'Come back d'you hear?'

Roland's tiny frame got to the sideboard and he ran under it into the darkness.

The Lady followed his move and smiled with satisfaction. She got down on hands and knees and crept ominously towards the sideboard.

Under the sideboard, in the inky darkness, Roland watched in fear as he saw the Lady approaching. He got right up to the wall skirting, and was about to despair, when Vein's voice popped into his mind, advising him: *There's a way out here somewhere, boy. If you can find it.*

Roland began to feel his way along the skirting board. He felt something that made him smile...

That's it! he thought.

The Lady pulled the sideboard back from the wall and her face showed her shock...

There, in the skirting board was a knot hole, just big enough for the miniature Roland to have squeezed through.

He had gone!

'Roland!' wailed the Lady, and then broke into sobs. 'Don't leave me – don't – don't!'

Roland was on the other side of the wall in the corridor. He looked back at the knot hole.

He could hear the strange woman calling to him from the room on the other side of the hole, 'Roland come back – please don't leave me. Oh, my baby, my poor boy! Don't go! We could have been so happy!'

Her voice sounded so heartbroken, that Roland began to think about going back to her.

But, after a few steps, he thought better of it. He turned around again...

Somewhere that Roland knew nothing of, in perhaps another dimension, events were going ahead which may have some bearing on Roland's strange journey, so far, far, away...

Vine with his torch, was leading the way down a dark staircase. He was backed up by Sergeant Tarr, who had June with him.

At the bottom, Vine stopped and turned to the others. 'Well, this is it. This is the sub-basement. This is as far as we can go. Sorry it's so dark, Mrs Wright, only I had to turn the power off, see?'

A very nervous June nodded uncertainly, 'Oh, yes.'

Vine shone his torch into a grille set in the concrete. He turned to Sergeant Tarr. 'Should be able to see the top of the lift cage through there.'

'Top?' said Sergeant Tarr, his brow furrowing.

'Gone right down to the stops, see.' Vine moved up the grille and shone his torch in. 'Gone down below floor level.'

Sergeant Tarr shook his head and sucked his teeth. He was not happy. 'Can you see anything at all in there?' he asked, stepping up on a breeze block to see in further.

June burst out crying, 'Oh Roland!'

Vine peered in. 'I'm looking now,' he said, then shook his head again.

June, imagining the worst, sobbed quietly to herself.

Chapter Four

Better this present than a past like that:
Back therefore to my darkening path again!

ROLAND WAS IN total darkness. He could hear the Lady crying, very faintly.

'Oh Roland... Don't go... Roland... Oh no!' her faraway voice was still calling.

He picked his way carefully down into the dark passage as he carried on, moving away from her. He reached the end but, to his dismay, was confronted with a grille that barred the way forward.

No way out, thought Roland, totally deflated.

Then, a flickering light, as if from a pitch brand, approached. It threw a wavering glow on the wall behind the grille. The light strengthened and Roland could now see Vein's huge face peering through the grille.

'Boy? Boy – you there?' called Vein.

'Over here, Mr Vein!' he shouted in his tiny, thin voice.

Vein held the torch higher and caught sight of Roland behind the bars, bathed in light.

'Go to your right, boy. Go to your right quickly!' he shouted urgently.

Roland did so and, still in almost total darkness, caught a glint of brass from a heart-shaped escutcheon plate. It was twice the size of Roland. There was a key in it but, from Roland's perspective, no sign of a door.

He put his tiny hand on the key and a feeling of hopelessness swept over him. As he realised that he couldn't possibly turn the giant iron key, Roland began to panic. How could he get out of this awful place? When would his nightmare end? He decided to try moving the key, but its weight was defeating his efforts.

Vein pushed the lighted brand nearer the grille, which gave Roland some light to see what he was setting about. 'Go on boy – you got it!' encouraged Vein. 'Now turn it with you.'

Roland looked back at Vein and muttered, 'All very well for you to say that.'

Even so, Roland addressed himself to the task and, using both arms, he managed to get a quarter turn. There was a pleasing, graunching noise from inside the lock. Then, putting all his weight on it, he managed to turn it around. There was a *click* as loud as a thunderclap. Encouraged, Roland pulled the key out of the lock. His knees buckled under the strain, but he bravely held on.

On the other side of the door, Vein was watching, holding the firebrand aloft. He saw the door with the heart-shaped lock swing open to reveal a full-size Roland emerging, with the key in his hand.

Roland was intensely relieved to be back as his normal size again. He took a few deep breaths.

'Lucky you got me lookin' out for you, eh boy?'

Lucky? Roland didn't answer Vein for a second, as his mind went over the weird things that happened to him over the previous few – minutes was it? Hours? Days, even? He certainly felt happier to be out of the Lady's room, and back in a reasonably familiar situation. Even though it meant he was stuck with Vein and his apparent help. Was Vein genuine? wondered Roland. Or was he somehow orchestrating Roland's strange journey? He felt it best to keep an open mind on the subject.

Roland pocketed the key and prepared to move on. However, he couldn't resist asking Vein the important question first. 'How?'

Vein regarded Roland with a completely expressionless face. 'How what?' he asked patiently.

'How did I get back to normal?'

Vein shook his head slowly and then went on, 'Normal! What's normal? How do you know what's normal and what's not? It's relative see. All relative.'

Roland began to form a question in his mind about relativity.

Vein anticipated it. 'And that's physics and that's nothing to do with me.'

'But you looked through the grille at me and the key,' Roland insisted.

Vein gave him that enigmatic grin which gave absolutely nothing away. 'Learning aren't you? Slowly – and that's what it's all about down here.'

'Why?' complained Roland, his frustration again rising to the surface. 'I never seem to learn anything useful.'

'What?' said Vein sharply. 'Still got your voice, haven't you? And your heart is still your own. Survived, haven't you? Struggled and survived through adversity. That's lessons learned in my book – and there's lots worse off than you.' Vein moved close to Roland and pressed his message home. 'As you may soon find out...'

This was a sobering challenge to Roland.

'Got the key, haven't you?'

Roland patted his pocket for the key, then took it out. When he looked up, Vein had disappeared. Only his disembodied voice hung in the air, echoing in the gloom: *Up you go, then.*

For the first time, Roland now saw a staircase leading up from the corridor. It seemed to invite him to climb to yet another floor. Yet another danger.

He looked down at the key without much enthusiasm, but moved to the stairs and laid his foot on the first step.

In that other world, Vine was shining his torch into the lift shaft. 'No... can't see a thing, too far down.'

'Why doesn't he answer? He must have heard us shouting,' said June, her voice croaked with tears.

Sergeant Tarr prepared himself to impart some of his thoughts on the situation. He cleared his throat then spoke to June. 'Well, have to face facts Mrs Wright. He could well have hurt himself in some way. Could be shock, or concussion or something.'

'Oh no,' said June with a shudder.

'Could be anything. We shan't know until we get him out, so the sooner the better, eh?' He gave her a flat non-committal smile.

She pulled herself together enough to nod at Sergeant Tarr.

Tarr turned back to Vine. 'Is there a manual system on these lifts?'

Vine nodded. 'Hand winch. Right up the top,' he said looking skyward.

'Come on then,' said Sergeant Tarr, marching off towards the steps, leading the others.

Roland Anthony Wright was ascending his own particular staircase. He began counting the steps in his head, for no particular reason.

... Sixteen, seventeen, eighteen, nineteen...

That's odd, he thought. Why nineteen and not twenty?

He reached a landing and come face to face with – the Warrior.

The Warrior struck a familiar Samurai pose. 'Wouldya?' he shouted. 'Staircase is Warrior's! So, Warrior's place –

Warrior's law! Must fight! Fight for life, you! Warrior must rule!'

Roland did his best to conceal his fear and answered the Warrior, in a quite matter-of-fact tone. 'Haven't done anything to you, have I?'

This was countered by a lightning stroke with the sword – checked just before it would have taken Roland's head off!

Roland backtracked, going down one step at a time.

The Warrior followed him making feint blow after blow. 'Ya... Fightya!' bellowed the Warrior.

Roland still managed to keep his voice loud and clear, with no wobbles in it. 'What do you want?' he asked.

'Rrunhh!' came the answer.

'But I haven't done anything to you, have I?'

'On a stairs! Stairs is Warrior's! So! Warrior's place – Warrior's law – must fight! Fight for life, you! Warrior must rule!' All this came over as a high-pitched battle cry.

Something made Roland decide to stick to his guns, and stick to his perfectly just question. 'But I've done nothing to you. What do you want?' he reiterated.

The Warrior yelled even louder. 'You fight, Warrior fight! Rule! Ruuuuuule!'

Roland backed down as his adversary slashed the sword at him. He got away from him, clattering down the steps to the next landing...

But there, sword at the ready, was the Warrior!

'Ya!' screamed the Warrior.

Roland swiftly ran back up the stairs again, but he could see the first Warrior still guarding the upper landing. Roland was sandwiched between two of them!

Then, Roland saw something that he hadn't noticed

before – a door in the half-landing. It was his only chance of escape. He tried to open it, but it was locked.

As he heard the Warrior from above coming down the stairs, he remembered that he had a key. Would it fit? He took it out of his pocket and tried it, then sighed with relief.

He opened the door, and dived through, just as the Warrior grabbed hold too. He tried to wrest the door away, but the Warrior was too strong. Roland let the door go and ran off along the new corridor beyond the door.

The Warrior followed in hot pursuit.

Roland found himself in a familiar place: the grille he had come though when he was tiny...

When the Warrior reached the grille, he caught only a glimpse of Roland – tiny again – making his way through the bars.

Clank! The Warrior slashed his sword down through the bars, trying to hit Roland. He was not quite fast enough. The tiny Roland had got through – but only just.

On the other side of the grille, Roland peered back at the Warrior. To his horror, the Warrior was now the same size as he was, and was after him again, still slashing away. It looked as if Roland would be transfixed by the sword until, at the last minute, he jumped – just as the Warrior lunged for the kill.

The jump took Roland into a dark space. As he went spinning round and round in the darkness, he knew he was getting bigger and bigger. The spinning stopped with a jolt and Roland was his normal size again, back on the opposite side of the grille. He looked down to see that the tiny Warrior looking through the bars of the grille, raging at him in a tiny voice! Roland backtracked to the door and picked up the key, then dashed up the stairs.

He moved cautiously until he reached a new landing, then stopped to listen for any sounds of pursuit. But other sounds intruded. There was the clatter of pots and pans, plates chinking in running water, and the dull thump of cleavers on chopping boards. Then, muffled and echoing, an adult's voice raised in anger, followed by the sound of a whiplash – and a child's voice, crying.

Roland advanced, slowly and carefully, as he listened to the strange medley of sounds. He noted that this new corridor had a more lived-in look about it. It was strewn with besoms, old wooden buckets and wicker baskets. Some were full of freshly-washed linen, while others held piles of dirty tablecloths and serviettes. He saw that the light no longer came from pitch brands. Instead there were hissing gas jets, which contributed to the strange feeling that he was in some kind of Victorian workhouse.

Roland came across a door. He hefted the key in his hand and wondered if he should try to open it. Then, from out of the shadows, a guard appeared. He was dressed in a black uniform, high-collared and brass-buttoned, with a cape and a stovepipe hat. Roland saw that he bore a certain resemblance to one of the policemen he had run from in the tower block – PC Briggs.

'Here!' the man barked. 'What are you doing with a key?'

Over by the lift doors, the two engineers were working on the door panel, under the supervision of Vowles. PC Briggs was still holding Ripper, hangdog beside him, when there was a beep and crackle from his personal radio. It caught the attention of Betty, Della and Alf, Ripper's gang.

PC Briggs answered his radio, *sotto voce*, 'Bravo sierra.' He paused, listening. 'Yes, Sarge, will do. Ambulance and fire service. Yes, Sarge. Yes. Over.'

There was a *shnick* as he turned the radio off.

The policeman had turned away on his call, to avoid causing any speculation, but everyone present had heard the words 'ambulance and fire service' and they reacted to what were now very serious matters.

PC Briggs moved over to the engineers, keeping Ripper alongside him. 'Possibility the kid's hurt,' he said. 'We want to winch the lift cage up, on manual.'

Hurdle, the older of the two engineers, made a face. 'We'll have to winch it up to here, then.'

'Why?' asked PC Briggs.

'Only doors open.'

Curry, the younger of the engineers, aped his mate. 'Only doors open,' he said. 'All the others are jammed shut.'

'The winch housing's upstairs. Right on top,' said Hurdle.

'Right up the top,' said Curry.

They all made a move for the stairs, PC Briggs still keeping Ripper with him.

'Need an Allen key an' all,' warned Hurdle.

'Allan key for the winch,' confirmed Curry.

PC Briggs snicked the radio button. 'India Romeo.'

A *schnick* again and Sergeant Tarr's voice could be heard. 'Go ahead, Bravo Sierra.'

'Sarge? A question of a key apparently.'

Roland was marched by the scruff, and thrust into a high-arched room with a stone-flagged floor. It had a Victorian, Gothic Revival feel to it. Roland noticed the smell immediately. It was soapy, mixed with stale food.

The room was lit by gas light and the only furniture was one desk and one chair – towards which Roland was being marched – where sat the Governor, who was dressed in black and bore an uncanny similarity to Sergeant Tarr.

Roland was roughly hauled in front of the desk.

The Governor said with some alarm, 'Key? What key? What was he doing with a key?'

'Trying to break into the chain locker, sir,' said the guard.

The Governor stood up and stared down at Roland. 'Do you know who I am, son?'

Roland had no idea, and was a bit dubious about the whole set-up. 'Policeman?' he ventured.

'Warden. Warden, Castellan and Governor of the Castle. Here to see things run smoothly. Without disruption. Know what disruption is? *You* are! Now, this key. Stole it, did you?'

Roland paused to select a reasonable sounding answer. 'No sir, I earned it.' He could see from the look on the Governor's face that he'd probably been a bit too pompous with his reply.

'Earned it? Earned it? You don't earn keys, son. You earn

promotion. By hard work and application. So, where did you get this key?'

'Found it, sir.' Roland decided to be as brief and enigmatic as possible – a plan that had worked for him before.

'Then I suggest you are a liar.'

'No sir.'

'I suggest that you are a liar as well as a thief!'

'No sir!' Roland's answer was bold and full of righteous indignation.

'You were found in possession of an implement with which you could attempt to break and enter Castle property, correct?'

Roland felt he couldn't get into a pointless round of accusation and denial. He decided to agree, to short circuit the whole business. 'Yes sir.'

'Good. Now, why?'

Ah, at last! thought Roland. Somebody who actually cared and wanted to know about his situation. 'I was trying to get out.'

'You were doing *what*?' said the Governor, glaring at him in total disbelief.

'Trying to get out. To escape.'

'Escape? To deliberately create disruption? You know what you are saying, son?'

Roland had been pushed as far as he could go and decided it was time to button his lips.

'How long have you been here?' asked the Governor.

Roland wanted to remain silent but words came pouring out instead, and he let go of all that was bottled up inside him in a burst of frustration. 'I don't know how long. I don't know why. I don't know where this place is and I don't care... All I do is go on and on! Nowhere on to nowhere, and nothing's ever normal! I get given keys – and then that's wrong. I'm here by mistake. The whole thing's a mistake, can't you see that? Of course I'm trying to get out, to escape, or whatever you want to call it. Surely *you* above all people, the Governor, you must see it's a mistake? I shouldn't be here. It's a mistake. Help me get out, please,' he implored.

There was a pause in which Roland actually became hopeful for a moment.

The Governor looked at him. 'You *are* here, so you *should* be here. There are no mistakes, and there is only one way out. Hard work. Understood?'

Roland's hopes were dashed and the hopeless, helpless feeling returned. 'Yes sir,' he said.

'Because of your offence, you start at the bottom,' said the Governor. He turned his eyes away from Roland and gave the order. 'Guard?' He nodded at Roland. 'Kitchens.'

The Guard took Roland in an arm grip. 'Restricted movement, sir?'

The Governor now had his nose in the book on the table, and didn't look up. 'Of course.'

Roland was led into a large circular room and told to wait.

As he waited, he looked at the huge frame that divided the room in half. It was festooned with hanging copper and iron pots and pans. One half of the room contained several large stone sinks, draining boards and buckets, above which were racks of drying clothes. The other half of the room was taken up with stoves and a spit, roasting irons and preparation tables.

Roland began to get concerned. He didn't like the look or

feel of the place. All too much work and no play, as far as he could work out.

At one end of the frame was an arch which seemed to have been converted into a dumb waiter, with a tray that was hauled up by ropes and pulleys. The dumb waiter sent prepared food up to whoever was on the receiving end and brought down empty, dirty dishes – that were immediately washed and dried, ready to be filled with food and sent up again.

Roland looked at the food going up, a nondescript stew of some sort, and wondered what exactly was going on upstairs. Some sort of restaurant maybe? Or an institution of some kind? Whoever it was up there, they certainly ate fast! The speed made it seem like an endless circle of pointless activity.

In the midst of it all was a Chef and a Sous Chef, working away frantically. They resembled Hurdle and Curry, the engineers from the tower block. Both men talked and sang non-stop, in a melange of English, French and Italian. Frangliano! Every now and then, without warning, they broke into snatches of romantic opera songs. The rest of the staff were children, frail skinny children, all of whom were chained to their workplace with neck collars, like slaves.

Roland began to feel distinctly unhappy about what his sentence might entail. He surveyed the not just busy, but frantic, kitchen and noted that the *plongeurs* (a word of French that he had actually learned, because he thought it was funny) doing the washing up, had longer and thinner chains that allowed them more movement to accomplish their work.

The Guard returned, carrying a long whip. He lashed out

at a child who was slacking, then turned to Roland. 'Right, my little thief. Now then. Best job is washin' up. The dumb waiter should be the worst... But it's not. That's your job.'

'Oh yes?' said Roland, not really wanting to know.

'You're the sweeper-upper. The collector of waste and any foodstuffs for recycling.' He led Roland by the collar to the cooking area, where the Sous Chef was cutting up cabbage and singing a snatch of *Tosca* at the same time.

As Roland entered, all the children-slaves turned their heads to stare at him.

The Guard cracked his whip above them. 'Get on with your work!' he shouted. 'On with your work! Work is Freedom!' He cracked the whip again just to emphasise his power over them and they immediately got back to work. 'Good. This is your new swabber. He's the lowest of the low and is to be treated as such!'

Roland noted the malicious reactions from the children.

'He's a thief,' the Guard added.

Delta, a girl, who seemed suspicious and afraid of everybody, clutched fearfully at the bag around her neck that contained all her possessions.

The Guard shoved Roland ahead of him as they passed her. 'Given to violence,' he said.

A very small boy, Alfie, totally petrified of physical punishment, hid himself from Roland.

The Guard pulled Roland up next to a girl called Beattie, who shrunk away from him. He guided Roland to a rack, where he clapped a heavy chain and huge iron ball to his ankle. 'Now boy, you work hard and give satisfaction – and in time you'll be promoted to a lighter chain. Won't he, Alfie?'

'Yes sir,' shouted Alfie.

The Guard stuck a bucket and mop in Roland's hands. 'And the harder you work, the better you'll get on. Work is Freedom!' he said, then stalked off, flicking his whip at those he felt were slacking.

Roland surveyed the organised chaos around him. He was unsure of what to do, what plans to make, but one thing was sure in his mind – he *must* escape somehow, and get out of the hell on Earth he had stumbled into. For now, he would watch and wait...

The dumb waiter came thundering down, the tray covered in a pile of crockery and half-eaten food. It was the signal for more furious activity to start.

Roland sank to his knees and started scrubbing the floor – not terribly energetically – in a place where he was able to keep an eye on the business going on around him.

The tray was carried over to the washing-up sink by two boys at the limit of their chains. The boys dumped the tray on the draining board. Beattie and Delta grabbed plates, dipped them in water, swished them around and wiped them. Bits of food and water splashed on the floor in front of Roland.

Bang! Clatter! Bang! went the plates into the racks.

Crash! One was dropped on the floor.

Crack! went the Guard's whip overhead.

'You clumsy baggage!' yelled the Guard.

Beattie flinched. With Delta's help, she banged the tray down in front of Alfie, who was washing and drying cutlery like a maniac.

He muttered under his breath as he did it. 'Knives and forks, knives and forks, forks and knives, knives and forks, spoons, spoons, spoons, knives and forks and knives and forks...'

Roland, still on his knees, was astonished by the massive operation. From the receiving to the washing up, the preparation, and the serving and despatch, it was a whirling cycle of seemingly endless toil.

As Roland reached the frame holding the pots and pans, he was confronted by a huge pile of vegetable debris that had come from the preparation table. He heard the machine-gun sound of the Sous Chef chopping cabbage, onions and carrots at spectacular speed.

The Sous Chef shoved another load of leaves onto the floor in front of Roland, then confronted him, addressing him in his Euro-blend tongue. 'Faster, faster, faster, obrigado! Subito. Vite, vite, vite, vite. Allez! Quick, unh?'

Roland swept up the huge pile, but he had no idea where he was going to put it. He shoved it past the Chef, a man with a waxed moustache, who was roaring out items from the order sheet.

'Quaranto six chicken au wine,' said the Chef.

The Sous Chef repeated the order. 'Six Coqinvin!'

'Two-a with-a mushroom!' boomed the Chef.

'Du champignon,' called the Sous Chef.

'Twenty-two pied-a-paquets, alla tripe!' the Chef replied.

'Vente due trotter, annna tripa!' echoed the Sous Chef.

Roland was amazed by their performance, but he found it didn't end there. Plates clattered onto trays to have food sloshed on to them, and the relentless cycle continued.

'Una tuna pie!' shouted Chef.

'Issa fora cat!' joked the Sous Chef.

'Seventy one coquille St Jaques!'

'Soixante onze scaloppini!'

'Fourteen spaghetti!'

'Quators pasta mia!'

'One hundred vichyssoise!'

'Centi zuppi!'

'Saltimbocca Roman style!'

'Bocca Romani!'

Roland looked at the food being served out. It was all a grey-brown coloured stew, he realised. Whatever dish was called out, it remained the same. He moved closer to the men, who continued their chorus.

'Cheeeken Marylang!'

'Witha cheeps!'

'Con Fritas!'

'Obrigado!'

'Essa nada!'

Roland watched another ladle-full of the stew slop poured onto the plates. 'Excuse me,' he said.

He got a quizzical look from the Chef.

The noise was such that Roland had to shout to make himself heard. 'Excuse me!'

The Chef looked down at him. 'What you want, whatsa trouble?'

'The food.'

The Chef glared at him. 'Whatsa wrong mit da food?'

'It's all the same,' said Roland incredulously. 'All of it.'

The Chef was obviously not used to questions and his expression changed to a defensive annoyance. 'Listen, Schluck. You do the sweeping an' I'll do the cooking – verstehen?'

'But you call it different names.'

'Si. So?'

'It's *stew*. All of it.'

The Chef's eyes narrowed. 'Whaddaya want? You! You tief! You steala my recipe!'

Roland soldiered on. 'What about the people eating it?'

'Whata people? Enh? Whatta you talk about? Nobody eats it!'

Roland's jaw dropped. 'Nobody eats it?' he said.

'Who'da wann eat this stuff? Eh? Itsa work! Work makes you free! Arebeit macht frie! You never heard that before?'

The Guard's whip lashed over their heads. 'No talking, you!' he shouted.

The Chef became very servile, bowing and ducking to the Guard. 'Sorry, Boss. I work, Boss. I work, tank you, Boss.'

Roland returned to sweeping the pile of garbage. He swept it towards the dumb waiter.

Two children were sending a tray of food up, after which a load of dishes came down. The uneaten food was scraped into a large metal bin on wheels. Then, to Roland's surprise, the kids fastened a harness strap over his shoulder. He realised that they wanted him to sweep and pull the bin along after him!

It's all stupid! Pointless and stupid! Ridiculous, pointless and *stupid*! he thought to himself. He was still looking for possible avenues of escape but he noted that the Guard was keeping a beady eye on his every move.

He carried on his round trip of the nightmare kitchen. Past the girls washing up and drying, then past Alfie, still doing his mantra, 'Knives and forks, forks and knives, knives and forks, spoons, spoons, spoons, knives and forks.'

He completed another full circle and came back to the

chefs again. He got the Sous Chef's attention and pointed at the wheeled bin. 'Where do I put this?'

'Just keepa sweepin.'

Suddenly, almost involuntarily, Roland's voice boomed out, giving vent to his angry thoughts about the crazy situation he found himself in. 'But that's pointless!' he shouted at the Sous Chef.

The Sous Chef kept his head down and answered, 'You're a sweeper. You sweep, okay?'

'What about this bin? Where do I put it?'

'In there.' The Sous Chef pointed to a large cauldron where he and the Chef cooked the stew.

Roland again gave vent to his anger and frustration. 'But that's pointless!'

'Itsa work,' said the Sous Chef.

'But it's *pointless*!' he shouted loud enough for everyone to hear. 'It's all pointless!'

The Guard blew a long shrill blast on his whistle.

Everyone in the whole place stopped instantly.

Roland noticed that they were all steadfastly staring at him. There was silence. Then, everyone except Roland sat on the floor.

He gathered his ball and chain and carried it over to where Alfie, Beattie and Delta were sitting.

'Why have you all stopped?' asked Roland.

Alfie, nervous as ever, put his hand over his mouth to talk to Roland. 'It's dinner time.'

'Nobody's eating,' observed Roland.

Then Delta piped up. 'Not s'posed to eat. S'posed to rest.'

Now Beattie laid down the law. 'Don't talk to him. Told not to talk to him. He's a liar and a thief. Only came down here to cause trouble. We were told not to speak to him.'

'D'you do everything you're told?' said Roland.

Beattie kept her mouth shut for a second or two, then said sharply. 'Yes... it's better.'

Delta, tears welling up, pleaded with Roland. 'Won't steal my jewels, will you?'

'Why should I?' said Roland, rather shocked she should think such a thing.

'Thief, aren't you?' said Beattie.

'They're all after my jewels. They're jealous,' said Delta.

Alfie winked knowingly at Roland to bring him into his confidence and said, 'They're not jewels really.'

Beattie crossed Alfie before he could say more. 'I told you not to talk to him. He'll get you into trouble. You know what'll happen then... They'll beat you!' She raised her hand to mime the whip.

'No, don't hit me,' whined Alfie.

'Can't you see?' continued Beattie. 'He's after your job, Alfie. Look at his chain – look at yours. How would you like to drag that great iron ball around? Hurt, wouldn't it?'

'Don't let him,' snivelled Alfie.

'What d'you mean?' snapped Roland. 'I don't want his rotten job.' He swivelled around to Delta. 'Or your jewels.'

'Want to cause trouble though don't you?' countered Beattie.

'What are you all so frightened of?' said Roland.

Beattie fixed him with her eyes and spoke in a raised whisper. 'You want to change things, don't you?' She looked at the other two for support. 'I know his sort. He says he'll make things better, but it's lies, he won't; he'll only make things different – not better. And I don't want things to be different. I want it all to be nice, all the same, day in-day out... the *same*.' She turned to Roland. 'So why don't you get back where you came from? Go on! Leave us be and get back where you came from!'

Roland regarded her patiently. 'Finished?'

She snapped her head away from his look.

He talked to the other two. 'I don't want your job, or your jewels. Or anything else. And I don't want to change things – you can all stay here and rot for all I care. Pointless boring waste of time! All I want to do is to get out. To escape.'

They didn't answer Roland immediately.

Alfie fiddled with his fingers, rubbing at the base of his ring finger as if trying to get rid of the grime he was working in. He didn't look up.

Delta bowed her head to avoid eye contact with him.

Beattie supplied their answer, in a very matter-of-fact kind of way. 'That's forbidden.'

'They beat you if you escape,' said Alfie in a quivering voice.

Delta chimed in, 'And they confiscate your things.'

Roland was saddened by their response and tried to figure out a way to get through to them. He tried a different tack. 'Look. Suppose you help me. Come with me, if you like.'

Beattie hissed at the other two, 'Don't listen to him.'

'After all,' Roland went on, 'how can they beat you or take your things away if you're not there? If you've gone?'

Roland waited for an answer.

Alfie supplied it. 'When they catch you...'

'Yes,' agreed Delta. 'They'll catch you.'

'Not me,' Roland said grinning at them. 'You want to

do this all your lives? Do you? You've been brainwashed haven't you? You're all scared, all scared of something... But what you're really scared of is freedom.'

Roland was cut off by the whistle blowing again.

They all stood up as one, and Alfie, Beattie and Delta said in unison. 'Work is Freedom!'

Almost immediately, the kitchen was working at full pelt again and the sound of clattering dishes filled the air.

Roland dragged his bin over to the Sous Chef's area.

The Sous Chef helped Roland tip the contents of the bin into the cauldron, then he dipped a spoon into the bubbling liquid and tasted it. He kissed his thumb and forefinger in appreciation and delight. 'Mnyaa!'

Roland was not keen to ask any more questions after the depressing results he'd had so far, but one thing did intrigue him and he decided to ask anyway. He scooped the last scrapings from the bin into the cauldron and then turned to the Sous Chef. 'Who's supposed to eat it anyway?'

A look of shock from the Sous Chef. 'You don't know?'

Roland shook his head.

'Why *El Supremo*. The Lord.'

Roland was confused, worrying that he might mean God in his heaven. That, he thought, would really be the last straw in this mad, mad world that he found himself in.

'Where?' said Roland tentatively.

The Sous Chef looked irritated, then clammed up and toed the party line. 'We justa cook. Send uppa da food, comprendo?'

Roland nodded towards the dumb waiter and turned his look up to the ceiling. 'Up there?' He watched the tray go up for the umpteenth time and said casually, 'So the Lord is up there somewhere, then?'

'Hey kid, why you askin' me all these-a questions? I don't know anything, only work here. Why you no work?'

The Chef intervened. 'Ey, you nogoodnik, make wida da broom. Allez, vite, vite, vite!'

As Roland swept away from him, he caught a glimpse of a familiar figure, concealed from the Guard's view behind a pillar. It was Vein, having a quiet cup of tea. He was holding the cup in a very genteel manner, thumb, forefinger and pinkie waving in the air.

As Roland came near, Vein gave him a toothy grin. 'Got you workin' have they?'

Roland wasn't interested in conversation and came right out with it. 'How did you get in here?'

'My own way. Always pop in for a cup of tea when I'm round this part.' He put on the grin again.

'How can I get out?' said Roland. He waited for Vein to come up with some kind of answer.

Vein moved his head slowly over towards the dumb waiter and gave the slightest of nods to Roland. 'Only one way, boy. Should've learned that by now.' His head moved again, this time up to the ceiling. 'Up. Always up.'

Roland started off on his round again. He moved slowly towards the dumb waiter, then stopped to pick up some garbage very near it, while making a careful check on how the mechanism worked.

The two boys working it stopped and looked at Roland suspiciously.

He could think of nothing to say, so he grinned and said lamely. 'Just, er, wondering how it works. Clever, isn't it?'

The boys didn't answer, but kept up a steady glare.

Roland moved on. He'd had enough time to gather that the dumb waiter could be worked from inside, by sitting on the tray and pulling on the ropes. He was pleased with himself and he began to feel better, now that he was planning to do something about his predicament.

Roland swept his way around the room and back to Beattie, who glared at him with furrowed brows, as if trying to work out what he was up to.

He smiled at her, which made her even more suspicious, and moved on, past the chanting Alfie: 'Knives and forks, knives and forks...'

Roland carried on sweeping his garbage into a huge pile, while he made a plan in his mind. His thoughts were halted by the sound of a huge crash, as a fully loaded dumb waiter full of dirty dishes hit the bottom.

Roland carelessly left his pile of garbage to watch the two boys at the dumb waiter sort out the plates. Then, he caught sight of the Guard and scampered back to his brush. He soon started sweeping again.

He swept round to where Beattie was standing. She looked Roland in the eye, then transferred her look to the Guard. He caught her meaning and nodded. He was beginning to feel that perhaps he'd found an ally in Beattie, despite all her angry talk. She definitely seemed to be trying to help him.

His warm thoughts were shattered when the Guard blew a long blast on his whistle.

Everyone in the room froze where they stood. Then, after a few seconds, there were murmurs, and soft whispered talk began to be heard.

Roland looked over at Delta. 'What is it? What's it for?'

'Teatime,' she whispered and looked at Beattie for approval. Beattie nodded, and the girls got 'tea' from the cauldron, by dipping their tin mugs in it. They sipped slowly.

Roland, having no mug, and pleased not to have to drink the sickly looking gruel from the pot, just sat near them.

Beattie gestured for Roland to position himself between Delta and Beattie, so that he couldn't be seen by the Guard.

He gave Beattie a gratified nod. 'Good!' He turned to the other two and whispered, 'Have either of you got a bit of wire? Hairpin or a brooch or anything?'

'She'll have something. She'll have something in her jewels,' said Alfie with a cruel smile.

Tears welled up in Delta's eyes. 'No, they're mine, you're not having any of them.'

Roland tried to placate her with a smile. 'Just let me see. I won't steal anything, honest. I'll give you something for it.'

'What?' said Delta.

Roland was stumped for a second, then replied, 'Let's see what you've got first.'

Delta thought about it for a while, then took her canvas bag off from around her neck. 'You're not to laugh or anything,' she said and cowered shyly.

Another cheery comment from Alfie, 'It's only what she finds in the food, see!'

Roland noticed that Beattie was listening to the conversation but trying, unsuccessfully, to look as if she wasn't.

Delta opened her bag.

Roland looked down at the pathetic collection of bits and pieces she called her jewels: Buttons, half earrings, a tiny buckle, bits of bracelet, a couple of marbles and a ball bearing. Then he saw a Kirby grip and picked it up. 'What do you want for this?' he asked.

Delta swiftly grabbed his hand with the Kirby grip in it. 'I said no stealing! One of my best ones that is. Give it back!'

Roland held up his other hand to quieten her. 'Look, I'll give you something for it. Something better.'

Delta snatched her bag and closed it. 'What?' she said.

Roland fished around in his pockets and found, half a ball pen, a few pence, string, a screwed up paper handkerchief, and a small whelk shell.

Delta looked at Roland and snatched the shell from him. 'I want this!'

'All right. You happy?'

'Yeah, it's nice, it's my best!' she said, admiring her new acquisition.

'Good,' said Roland. 'Now keep a lookout for me.'

Alfie and Delta looked out for Roland in all directions as he attempted to pick the lock on his ball and chain with the hair grip.

Beattie got the attention of the Guard and nodded her head for him to come over to her.

In response, the Guard started to move down the stair, towards them...

Roland stopped what he was doing.

'Look out!' said Alfie under his breath.

Roland went into frozen mode and tried to prepare some kind of riposte.

The Guard passed by Roland and spoke to Beattie. 'On your feet, you. Governor wants to see you.'

'What for!' cried Beattie. 'I haven't done anything!'

The Guard unlocked her chain and, when she was free, pushed her towards the stairs.

Beattie went forward unwillingly, in front of the Guard, speeding up when he cracked his whip behind her.

'Go on! Up the stairs!'

When she had gone, Roland turned to the others. 'That's lucky,' he said.

'No it isn't,' said Alfie sharply. He looked scared to death.

Roland noted that Delta too was quaking with fear. 'She always does that. She always goes to see the Governor, when she's telling on us!'

'I'd better hurry up then!'

Alfie grabbed hold of Roland's arm in fear. 'She'll tell him I helped and they'll beat me.'

'You haven't helped as much as I have. Has he?' said Delta.

Roland was concerned about Beattie, but he could only imagine what was going on in the Governor's office.

Would Beattie really tell, he wondered, and put them in danger?

Sadly, at that very moment, Delta's words were coming true...

In the Governor's office, a frightened Beattie was standing before the Governor, who was still scribbling figures in his ledger book.

'Yes?' he said, not looking up. 'And then what?'

Beattie was tearful, tremulous, scared of her master. 'And he said it was pointless.'

'Go on.'

'Said we'd been brainwashed. We were all scared. Said we

should all riot. And then he said we should all be free – but work *is* freedom, isn't it?'

The Governor nodded and spoke without looking up, 'Then?'

'Then he said we had to help him escape, and he made the other two do it. But I wouldn't, sir. I don't want things changing all the time, getting all disrupted.'

Beattie obviously knew the Governor's way of thinking. At these words, he stood up abruptly, raising his shoulders. 'Disruption is it? He must be stopped.'

The Governor picked out his favourite whip from a rack and led Beattie and the Guard out of his office...

In the kitchens, Roland was still struggling to open his manacles. At last, there was a loud tick, the lock sprung open, and he was free.

He jumped to his feet as the Governor, the Guard and Beattie started to descend the stairs. Turning to Alfie, he said, 'I'll need you to help me when the time comes, Alfie. I'll call you. All right? Don't forget, will you?'

'But they'll beat me,' Alfie said, with a sob.

Roland dashed off towards the dumb waiter.

'Stop him! Stop that boy!' screamed the irate Governor.

The two cooks barred Roland's way to the dumb waiter.

Roland glanced at the Guard, coming at him from the direction of the staircase, then ran across the room – closely followed by the Chefs. He jumped onto the table and pushed the frame full of pots and pans into their path. There was a huge crashing and smashing noise. Plates and pots rolled all over the place and the Chefs went sprawling onto the floor, where they were trapped by the frame.

Roland was pleased, but he still had to deal with the Guard, who was approaching him from behind the frame. He pushed the wheeled bin at the Guard, who tried to avoid it but tripped on some pottery debris and fell to the floor.

Suddenly the stentorian voice of the angry Governor rang out close to Roland, 'Stop him! This is disruption! Anarchy! Chaos! Get him!' He lashed out at Roland with his whip.

Roland managed to get behind the cauldron just in time.

The other children were all too scared to do anything but cower, utterly fascinated by Roland's single-handed rebellion.

'Come back here!' shouted the Governor.

With one huge effort, Roland tipped the cauldron over, spilling the steaming swill on the floor. The Governor tripped and fell and splashed into the muck. He was covered in the stuff!

Roland continued his effort to get to the dumb waiter.

Alfie was watching, totally mesmerised by the events going on around him.

Roland's voice called to him urgently, 'Now Alfie! Now!'

Alfie registered it and whimpered, 'But they'll beat me.' Then, despite himself, he carried out Roland's orders. He ran towards the dumb waiter, getting around the Chefs, the Guard who was nursing his ankle, and finally the Governor – speechless and covered in the sludge from the cauldron.

The Governor slipped about, trying in vain to clear his eyes of the stuff, as Roland watched Alfie's approach.

Roland climbed into the dumb waiter. 'Well done, Alfie. Now, help me pull! Pull on the rope!'

'They'll beat me. I know they will!' moaned Alfie.

Roland hauled from inside, but wasn't strong enough

to haul his weight on his own. 'Pull, Alfie!' he urged. He turned to the other two boys at the pulley. 'And you two! Pull!'

After a slight hesitation, the two boys started pulling too.

Buoyed up by this, Roland called to the whole kitchen, 'What have you got to lose? Nothing! Not even your chains! Come on. Pull!'

Other boys and girls made a move to the dumb waiter to watch Roland slowly being hoisted up. Several others took the ropes – even Delta joined in.

Roland started to chant. 'Pull together! Pull together! Pull! Pull! Pull!'

With the added effort, Roland and the dumb waiter ascended into the darkness of the shaft.

Roland wondered where this journey would take him next, what world he might find himself in. A chink of light above him told he would soon find out.

In the world lost to Roland, two pairs of hands were pulling a metal handle down. There was the clickity-clack sound of a ratchet as the lever was pulled rhythmically, backwards and forwards, backwards and forwards, causing a steel cable to wind itself – agonisingly slowly – around a drum.

The work was being done by the two engineers, jerking the emergency hand winch. They were watched in silence by PC Briggs, Ripper, Vine, Sergeant Tarr, and Voss – now bespectacled and poring over the lift's instruction manual as the engineers sweated away at the winch.

The scene was illuminated by a single dim light bulb.

Curry stopped working, took several deep breathes and complained, 'Goin' to take all night at this rate.'

Hurdle, too, took deep breaths and leaned on the winch handle. 'And all bloody day.'

Their complaints met with silence. So, after a short rest, they continued to manhandle the lift up the shaft, until a graunching, scraping noise was heard. The lift cage had hit some kind of obstruction. They tried, but could not move the winch.

'He's stickin' somewhere,' said Hurdle.

They made another effort to get it moving but it seemed to be stuck fast.

'Stuck,' said Hurdle solemnly.

Roland was sitting on the dumb waiter platform, moving faster and faster upwards, towards possible freedom. Suddenly, he felt a sudden massive jolt, and the dumb waiter stopped with such force that Roland was propelled off the platform into darkness.

Roland rolled out onto a floor and found himself in a small grey room. It was very high and narrow, with no doors or windows, no furniture, nothing. Just a bare, cold room.

Roland stood up slowly, and took in his surroundings yet again. Another weird place, he thought, a chill running up his spine at the thought what might come next.

Then, a loud, accusative, disembodied voice shook the room and filled Roland with fear...

'Roland Anthony Wright. You have gone as far as you can.'

Chapter Five

I shut my eyes and turn'd them on my heart.
As a man calls for wine before he fights...

THE LIFT ENGINEERS were trying desperately to free the cable, to no avail.

Curry finished a last pull on the lever. 'Far as he'll go, Mr Voss.'

Hurdle confirmed the bad news, 'Yes, that's as far as it'll go.'

'Perfectly simple explanation. Question of procedure, that's all,' said Voss. He leafed through his manual, trying to find some instructions for their predicament.

Sergeant Tarr hesitated before asking, 'Can't we get an expert in?'

Voss turned to face the sergeant, looking none too happy.

'Sergeant, I am maintenance supervisor. We've had these problems before. It's just a matter of maintaining priorities and establishing procedure before we start.'

He was met with a steely stare.

Voss decided to assert his authority. He started waving his hands to shoo everyone away. 'You know, it would help if you could clear the area. We can't work in these conditions,' he complained.

'Right, Briggs, do as the – ah – supervisor says,' said Sergeant Tarr.

PC Briggs obeyed his order and moved the knot of people around the corner.

Sergeant Tarr turned to Voss and pressed home the point. 'Mr Voss, there's a boy down there, you know. Won't forget, will you now?' With a nod in salute, he left to join the others.

Roland looked around carefully to find out where the voice had come from. He settled on a point high on the wall, and addressed it. When he spoke, there was a new-found resilience present in his voice. 'What d'you mean, I've gone as far as I can go? I want to get out! Isn't there anyone here who understands that?'

Roland waited, and heard the click of an intercom being turned on.

An answer came in another voice. 'Of course you do. And we are here to help you. If there are any delays, please be patient. Your application is being processed and we are doing all we can, within the limits of the system.'

It was a male voice: calming, bland and apparently caring, but Roland could tell it was speaking pure Public Relations blather.

There was a pause and the voice turned steely, 'Please stay exactly where you are. Thank you.'

With a click, the intercom was switched off.

'But where am I?' bellowed Roland to the emptiness around him.

Another pause and click before the voice replied, 'Someone will be along to see you shortly.' *Click.*

'Hey you!' shouted Roland, angrily. 'Hello! Hello! Hello!' He exhausted himself shouting and paused for breath.

Suddenly, he found Vein standing beside him.

Vein spoke softly, as if to emphasise his message. 'Hello boy,' he said. 'Not supposed to shout in here. This is a waiting room.' He gave a superior lift of his head to the ceiling.

'What?' Roland wasn't exactly pleased to see Vein, but had expected to come across him again at some time or another. 'It's you again.'

A flat smile from Vein. 'Done well for yourself, you have. Practically at the top now, you are. Pleased, are you?'

'Not particularly,' retorted Roland, then with sarcasm creeping into his voice, 'Only a room, isn't it? No doors, no windows, Nothing special about that, here.'

'Now look here, don't go getting too high and mighty, Master Roland. Try a bit of patience. You'll need it, now you're in the Bureau.'

'What bureau?'

Vein took a breath to answer, but the soothing voice came

over the intercom, interrupting them. 'Roland Anthony Wright, please.'

Roland turned to Vein, but he had gone. Where he'd stood there was a key, a chrome-plated Chubb type.

Vein's voice came to Roland, drifting across the ether, 'Patience, boy. Patience and cunning.'

Roland stooped down and picked up the key. To his surprise, when he rose there was a door right in front of him. He put the key into the lock...

Roland stepped through the door and found himself in a corridor lined with desks. The desks were in a round-cornered Thirties style, and each one was manned by a Bureau officer in a light grey suit, with a huge pile of cardboard files in front of him. The officers were well groomed, but the hotchpotch of other men and women in the room were all quite shabbily dressed. They were the supplicants waiting to be seen. Roland had touched on the Jarrow March in his History lessons at school, and felt that the supplicants were dressed quite similarly to the pictures he had seen – in old Macs, overcoats and caps.

The voice called Roland's name again. 'Roland Anthony Wright?'

Roland quickened his step and strode down the corridor.

'Calling Roland Anthony Wright!' the voice said again, a little louder this time.

Roland walked past desk after desk, all heaped up with files. The whole set-up felt as if it belonged to an organisation which had grown so large that it had overflowed out of its offices and into the corridors. Roland passed desks where forms were being filed in and questions gently, but persistently, asked. He passed more desks, then more and more, until he started to wonder when he would find out where he was supposed to go.

The voice came on the intercom again. 'Roland Anthony Wright to cubicle 4-0-6-7 please.'

Suddenly, he came face to face with a glass partition made from reeded opaque glass. On it, in a Thirties-style typeface, was the number 4067.

Roland poked his head around the partition.

Behind it, he found a pale, thin-faced, balding man – aged about fifty, to Roland's reckoning. He very closely resembled Mr Voss, the maintenance supervisor from back home. Roland noted the line of pens stuffed into the man's top pocket, like soldiers lined up. The plaque on the desk informed Roland that the man's name was Voysey.

The man glanced up at Roland. He had an intelligent face, and looked a bit like a senior civil servant. He was totally surrounded by towers of files, not only on his desk, but all around on the floor and any other space that would take them. 'Roland Anthony Wright?' he asked. His voice was certainly the same as the one Roland had heard in the waiting room.

'Yes,' said Roland, delighted to feel that at last he was getting somewhere.

'Do sit down.'

Roland looked at the files on the chair, and moved them to the floor, before sitting down and looking up at Voysey.

Voysey smiled as he checked Roland against the file he had been perusing. Satisfied, he closed the file and placed it in the 'Pending' tray. He then linked his fingers into an arch and looked at Roland, the smile fading from his lips. 'Now. What is it, exactly, that you want?'

Roland regarded Voysey seriously, then said with heavy emphasis, 'To get out.'

Voysey leaned back in his swivel chair. 'I see. This is your first application?'

'Yes,' said Roland.

Voysey held his hand out, as if he was hoping to receive something. 'Your application form? Can I have it please?'

'I haven't got one,' replied Roland, noting that Voysey was beginning to twitch around the corners of his mouth.

Voysey suddenly took on the appearance of a man at the end of his tether, a bureaucrat and servant who was – only just – keeping the lid on it all. 'Oh dear, oh dear,' he said, disappointed. Then his tone sharpened. 'Why?'

'I've only just got here.'

'Why didn't you come here first?'

'Because I've been to all the other places.'

'But didn't they tell you about the application form?'

'No,' said Roland.

'Well, honestly, they should have. There's nothing I can do without an application form. You can see the conditions I have to... It's deplorable, honestly. If –'

Roland cut off his self-pitying rant. 'Where do I get one?'

'Mr Voysey.'

'You're Mr Voysey,' said Roland incredulously.

Voysey shook his head and said, '4-0-3-3.'

Roland went out into the corridor again to seek out cubicle 4033. He hurried past the desks, then became more relaxed as he spied cubicle 4034.

The next one he saw was 4032. Then 4031...

He retraced his steps and poked his head around 4032, where the officer and his supplicant were talking in hushed tones.

The officer looked up at Roland 'Yes?'

'Where's 4-0-3-3?'

The officer shook his head as if to say, *not again*. Then, with a forceful, rather ratty, tone he said, 'Behind you!'

'Thanks,' said Roland. He about-turned and there, right in front of him, was a small sliding panel in the wall with the number 4033 on it. He knocked on the panel and waited.

The panel was raised and Roland found himself facing Voysey again – only now the man was wearing a very obvious false moustache, the kind that might be used at a fancy dress party.

'Yes?' enquired the now-moustachioed Voysey.

'I...' Roland recognised Voysey but thought better than making a point of it. 'I need an application form.'

'What for?' came the reply.

'To apply,' said Roland calmly.

'I see. Could I have your card?'

Roland's calm was quickly turning to anger. 'What card?' he asked tersely.

'The one you need for the form.'

Roland suppressed his anger, just. 'Where do I get the card?'

'From Mr Voysey. 4-0-8-5.'

Roland, with anger rising, went to cubicle 4085 and put his head around the glass. 'Mr Voysey?'

There was Voysey again, this time with a false beard and thick glasses. 'Yes?'

'I need a card for the application form.'

'Pink, green or buff?'

Roland's eyes rolled, but he was determined to keep it up, determined not to let the stupid system beat him. He would take all the mad, bureaucratic, garbage they could throw at him!

He ended up with a sheaf of papers. He marched back to the original Voysey in cubicle 4067, and plonked the papers in front of him. 'Okay?' he said.

Thankfully, Voysey began to study them and spoke as he read. 'You wish to make application for an exit permit?'

'Yes.'

Voysey wrote Roland's full name on a form. 'Roland... Anthony... Wright... Purpose for exit?'

'To visit relatives,' said Roland. He was pleased that he'd chosen to answer with an obvious, simple reason, one that could hardly be challenged.

Voysey looked up again. 'Length of stay?'

Roland had to take a punt here. 'As long as necessary.'

He got a sharp glance from Voysey. 'Qualifications?'

Again Roland's mind raced to think of a good answer. Then he had a brainwave. 'Er... student.' He was only sure the answer had been accepted when he was asked the next question.

'Have you ever been in trouble with the authorities?'

Roland looked him right in the eye. 'Never.'

Voysey looked up at Roland and then down to a thick file bearing Roland's history. It had his name stencilled on it: Wright, RA. 'Are you *sure*?' asked Voysey.

'Positive.'

'How long have you been with us?'

'Some time.'

There was an exchange of false smiles.

Voysey then picked up the dossier on Roland. He placed it on his desk and patted it with both hands. 'You do realise that this file contains a detailed account of your activities since you came here?'

'Oh.'

'Yes,' said Voysey. He started flicking through the pages with utter distaste. 'Mmm... Not pleasant reading, is it? Destruction, heartbreak, chaos.' He sighed. 'And now this.' He waved the forms he'd filled in at Roland. 'Tissue of lies from start to finish.' He looked at Roland sternly. 'You and your application are rejected!' He slammed a big rubber stamp across the file, and the word REJECTED appeared in three inch letters all the way across it. 'Next!'

'What do I do now, Mr Voysey? What do I do now?'

Voysey ignored him completely. 'Next!'

Roland knew he'd been dismissed. He left and passed the next supplicant going in... Then noticed that the next supplicant was Vein, with a sheaf of forms all ready.

Roland felt that Vein was looking a bit too pleased with himself. He snapped at him, 'Now what?'

'You got to go direct.'

'Who to?'

'The Lord of the Castle, who else?'

At Brandon House, in that other world...

Sergeant Tarr, PC Briggs, Ripper, Vine and June listened to the banging and clanking from the lift shaft as the engineers worked on it.

A figure came running up the stairs. It was Ron, carrying his sax case and still wearing the toggle hook around his neck. It bounced to and fro as he ran.

When he saw June he ran to her. They embraced, she holding him tighter than he'd like and thus worrying him more. 'What's all this about, love?'

'Oh Ron!'

'What's going on?' Ron looked around, seeking a figure of authority. He looked back at June and said in a slightly accusative, aggrieved tone, 'Honest, love. They pulled me right out of the gig. Right in the middle of a set. Where is he? Where's Roland? What's happened?'

Sergeant Tarr moved towards him. 'Mr Wright?'

Still stung by events, Ron moaned to Sergeant Tarr as well, 'Right in the middle of the gig, man. Pulled me right out. What happened, Officer?'

'Seems your boy's stuck in the lift, Mr Wright.'

'Eh? Stuck in the lift? I thought he must have been run over or something. I mean, you get pulled out of the gig like that – you think, you wonder, don't you? Is he all right?'

Sergeant Tarr laid a hand on his shoulder and led him away, just out of June's hearing. 'The engineers are working on it now.' He lowered his voice and continued. 'We can't get him to answer.'

Ron frowned, only just beginning to grasp the gravity of the situation. 'What?'

Sergeant Tarr continued. 'I haven't said anything to Mrs Wright, but there seems to have been a bit of a knife fight.'

'What?' Ron's voice was now full of concern.

'And it's possible he may have got hurt...'

Ron's reaction was one of complete shock.

Roland found himself in another place, lying face down on the floor in a darkened area beyond the desks. The floor was red and wet, and for a second it seemed like it could be blood...

Roland could hear a voice from a way off.

'Think he must have hit his head against a brick wall, or something.'

He recognised it as Vein's. Roland moved his eyes towards the sound and saw Vein and Voysey, plus a few of the ragged old supplicants, standing over him, looking down.

Voysey was very unhappy and irritated that his work has been interrupted. 'Oh there, you see? I can't be expected to deal with this sort of thing as well; I'm snowed under as it is!' He gestured to the supplicants behind him. 'I've got people in serious need of assistance here.' He looked around for a way out, then shouted, 'Guards! Guards!'

Two muscle-bound security guards in black uniforms made their way towards Voysey.

He turned to them. 'Bit of a problem here. Get rid of it will you?'

The guards hoisted Roland up by the shoulders.

When Roland was upright, he was just level with their shoulder flashes, which he noted were of a castle on a spiral background, with a crown on top, and two bearers – a knight with a sword, and a woman with a lyre.

He looked down and saw a bottle of red ink roll out from underneath him, dribbling the rest of its contents on the floor. That accounted for the 'blood'.

Vein adroitly concealed it from the security guards. As they hauled Roland off, he picked the ink bottle up and read the label: RED INK. PROPERTY OF THE BUREAU.

Roland thought he must have passed out. He heard a door slam shut and opened first one eye, then the other, and found that he was in a long narrow room. There was a small door at one end, and double doors at the other, with the Castle's coat of arms above them. A red carpet ran across the room from one end to the other.

He suddenly realised that he was lying on a plush chaise-longue. It was quite dark, but he could see no other furniture in the room. He still felt a little woozy from his fall, so he took deep breaths to clear his head, knowing full well that he would have to be alert to figure out what was what in the bizarre world he now inhabited.

He heard the sound of footsteps and the mumbling of voices, and hurried over to the double door where the sounds were coming from. He placed his ear against the door and listened.

'He insisted on seeing you m'lord, one way or another.'

'Why me? Why me, Vein? They think I've got nothing else to do?'

The room through the double doors was the Great Hall, a place lit by pitch brands. The walls were draped in flags, and suits of armour adorned each corner. The floor was on three different levels, leading steadily up to the plinth on which the throne stood.

The Lord of the Castle, who bore a heavy resemblance to Roland's dad, was seated on the throne with one leg cocked over the arm rest. The throne was an ornate gothic affair with loads of lavish gold filigree over it.

The Lord's clothes vaguely resembled Ron's band outfit. He wore a frothy white embroidered shirt with big puffy sleeves, a black velvet waistcoat, a floppy black velvet bow tie, and a red cummerbund over black velvet trousers, which were tucked into high boots. The Lord looked a bit like Hamlet as a bandleader at the Locarno. A tape player was fastened to his cummerbund, with a lead to an earpiece in his crown, which had stereo pots fitted to it. It was hanging on the corner post of the throne, the faint of tinny sound of music issuing from it.

The Lord was posed sloppily over the throne, vaguely aware of Vein but not really interested in what he had to say. His ear and thoughts were concentrating on the music coming from the pots...

'He thinks you're the only one can sort him out, you see,' said Vein, who was bent slightly forward in deference to the Lord.

'What do these people think I do all day? Bugging me all the time.'

'You are the top man, m'lord,' said Vein.

'Right! Exactly. I keep the show on the road, right? Takes a lot of organisation. What about *my* work? When do they think I get to do that?'

There was a quizzical look from Vein as he raised his head to look at the Lord. 'Your – work, Sire?'

The Lord popped on his coronet with the built-in speakers, effectively cutting himself off from everything around him. 'Can't you see I've got a stack of material to listen to?' He listened intently, eyes closed totally, abstracted by the music.

With a hint of warning in his tone, Vein raised his voice and said, 'He'll get to see you somehow, Sire. He's that type. Set on it, he is. He's come all the way up from the dungeons, from bottom to top.'

The Lord caught some of Vein's speech. It made him concerned enough to interrupt his listening for a second to say, 'You think I'm at the top? Let me tell you something, Vein, something about the pyramid of power... Hang on.' His concentration returned to the music momentarily. 'Yeah! Cool!' The Lord chimed in with the final crescendo – 'Baa-dah-did-um-baah!' – then he returned to his hard-done-by theme. 'They all think I'm sitting at the top doing nothing, lording it over everybody. Well, I'll tell you, it's the bloody wrong way up, mate. They're all weighing down on me!' He pointed at himself. 'This is the point of the pyramid here! Right here, man!' He pointed down on the top of his head and mimed holding a heavy weight above him. 'And I'm holding it all up, Vein. You dig?'

Having said his piece, the Lord returned to his listening.

Outside, in the anteroom, Roland felt like he had been locked out of any control of his destiny. Ever since he'd got here, he had just been pushed from pillar to post, told to this and told to do that. And now, he was in the anteroom of some Lord or other.

A Lord! he thought scornfully. Why should anyone have

that kind of power over other people? It was just plain wrong to his mind. Why can't we just get on with each other? Why the eternal struggle? He, for one, wasn't having it any more...

Roland stood square on to the double doors and ran at them.

He burst into the Great Hall at a rush, then brought himself to a halt as he saw that the place was empty. The only noise he could hear was coming from the crown, resting high up on the throne, emitting its tinny music through the earphones. Roland suddenly felt terribly alone in the huge room.

He pulled himself together once more and decided to make a tour of the Great Hall. He strolled up to the throne and inspected it, then examined the crown from which the music came. As soon as he touched it, the music started to sound more ominous, with a tinkling Japanese touch to it... Roland felt the hairs on his neck go up. He looked around, then his eyes went up to the gallery.

There, watching him, was the Lord.

The Lord moved into the shadows as soon as he saw Roland's gaze turned in his direction.

Roland walked about the hall, causing huge shadows from the flaming pitch brands to flare up the walls. He heard a noise and looked behind him. 'Vein?' he called. 'That you? Where are you?'

Vein had concealed himself behind a pillar. He was watching, but saying nothing.

Roland called out to the room. 'Vein! I want to see the Lord of the Castle. This Lord of yours – where is he?'

In another circumstance, in another mental dimension, other souls were trying to understand their own reality...

Ron was staring, slightly agape, at Sergeant Tarr as he spoke.

'And that's it sir. He's stuck down there, and all the doors are jammed but this top one. We're having trouble with the hand crank. Plus, there's the fact that he's not answering.'

Ron looked more worried as he took it all in.

'Oh,' added Sergeant Tarr. 'I've put out a call for an ambulance.'

'Yeah, well... Thanks,' said Ron in a daze. He gave a bitter smile. 'Kids! What can you do? Can't be there every minute of the day, can you? I mean, we've all got work to do.'

Sergeant Tarr looked at Ron's saxophone case. He obviously had his own thoughts about what 'work' was. Work, *real* work, was what he did on the Force – not playing daft music to excite kids until they started fights; fights which were the very place that Sergeant Tarr's work started in earnest.

Ron nodded at Ripper. 'What does he say about it?'

'Not much,' said Sergeant Tarr, not wanting to reveal anything before any blame attached to anyone.

Ron moved over to PC Briggs who was still holding Ripper. He went straight up to the lad and spoke into his face. 'You pleased, are you? Pleased with what you've done?'

'I didn't do nothin'. He started it,' exclaimed Ripper.

'Oh yeah? He just came up and attacked you, did he? One small lad? On to you and your mates?'

Ripper just shrugged.

It was the sort of cheeky amused shrug that made Ron want to pulverise the boy. He pointed his finger at Ripper and said, 'Listen, you, if you've hurt my kid...'

'Never touched him,' said Ripper, getting in fast.

PC Briggs intervened. 'That's enough. All right? Both of you.'

June, who'd heard Ron's accusations, put her hand on him. 'Ron, don't.'

But he held her off. 'Hang on, June.' He addressed Ripper again, 'Did you?'

'Told ya, didn' I? Never touched him.'

Sergeant Tarr arrived to quell the fire, with a mild rebuff to Ron. 'That'll do, Mr Wright.'

Ron allowed June to pull him away.

Sergeant Tarr told PC Briggs, quietly, to remove Ripper, before there was any more trouble.

Roland's frustration was building as he crept around the Great Hall looking for Vein and the elusive Lord. They seemed to be playing cat-and-mouse with him, just wishing to keep out of his way.

Roland's attention was taken up by a suit of armour, when he heard a sound behind him. He whipped around. 'Vein?'

He moved to where he thought the sound had come from and approached the throne dais.

But the Lord was lurking in the gallery above him, looking down on him, watching...

Roland searched the flickering shadows, then backed towards the gallery stairs.

Vein was watching his every move too.

'Vein! Answer! I know you're here!' yelled Roland. He stopped to listen.

Nothing...

Then the shuffle of feet.

Roland backed right up to the staircase, and turned to face the stairs.

Up in the gallery, the Lord moved into shadow, out of sight.

Roland decided to climb the stairs. He put one foot on the first step...

At once, there was a thump of feet hitting the floor and the Warrior appeared at the top of the stairs. 'Wouldya!' he screamed. He started to descend, striking Kendo-type attitudes on every step.

Roland backed away into the hall and the Warrior followed, shouting as he slashed the air with his vicious looking sword. 'You make a fool ofa Warrior? Wouldya? Now is Warrior's revenge. Yehhh! Fight ya!'

The sword whistled past Roland's nose and he started to run.

The Warrior pursued him in and out of the pillared arches, screaming his challenge, slashing at every opportunity with swipes that – had they connected – could well have bisected Roland!

'Fightya! Showya what you get you make fool of Warrior. Warrior rule!' The Warrior took a flailing swipe between each threat. 'Warrior rule!' *Slash!* 'Warrior rule!' *Slice!* 'Warrior Rule!' *Swipe!*

Roland used a large pillar to keep him out of slashing range. By going round and round the pillar, dodging the Warrior's onslaught, he found himself in a position of comparative safety.

Roland decided to try and reason with the Warrior. 'Listen!'

Clang! The sword connected with the pillar right beside Roland.

He quickly moved on around the pillar and tried again. 'Look, I've got no quarrel with you! All I want...'

Blang! The Warrior's slash was close.

Roland battled on, '... is to get out. Get to the top! I want to see the Lord!'

Klang!

'The Lord of the Castle!'

'You wanna see alord! You got to pass me first! None can see the Lord! Lord see none! None shall pass Warrior! Yahhh! Fightya!'

The onslaught caused Roland to take up another defensive position. This time he sought cover behind a suit of armour.

The Warrior was in close pursuit – too close!

Roland shoved the suit of armour into him.

The Warrior was tangled up in it for a while, yelling as he tried to free himself.

Roland dashed to another suit of armour and had just enough time to take the sword and helmet from it. He quickly placed the helmet on his head and lowered the visor, then he struck a pose, his beautiful broadsword held in a defensive position. 'Listen!' screamed Roland, but before he could utter another word, he was in a sword fight.

Slash! Bang! Crash!

Even as he fought, Roland continued his diplomatic offensive, begging the Warrior to listen to his plea.

The fight gathered momentum as Roland began to give as much as he'd taken. He jumped up onto the plinth, which gave him a height advantage over the Warrior. Suddenly, Roland saw himself as the great avenger. He was like one of the characters he read about in his precious comics. He was the underdog against a mighty aggressor. He was Captain America! Thor! One of the Fantastic Four! David against Goliath! Asterix against the Romans! He was Saint George fighting the dragon...

Even with his morale boosted with thoughts of his heroes, Roland was forced from his place of height advantage, back down to floor level. The Warrior chased him around a refectory table with candles on it. Their light threw fantastic shadows onto the cloister walls.

Roland made a defensive swipe at the Warrior's swinging sword and sliced the top off the candles.

He picked up a chair to ward off his assailant, but with a wild slash, the Warrior chopped its legs off with one blow...

Roland moved backwards around the table, still holding his enemy at bay.

The Lord was enjoying every minute of the fight, as he looked down from the balcony.

Vein, too, was watching, but he seemed a little more

alarmed whenever the duelling got close to him. He was able to stay out of danger by keeping on the move, hiding behind curtains.

On his second rotation of the table, Roland snatched the tablecloth off and spilled all the dishes, bowls and jugs onto the floor.

The Warrior couldn't stop the aggressive advance he was making and crashed into the debris. It unbalanced him. He fell to the floor but, before Roland could take advantage, he was up again.

Roland used the tablecloth like a Roman Retarii gladiator used his net: he threw it over the Warrior and got him tangled up in it. Then he moved in and landed a blow on the Warrior...

The Warrior gave a roar of pain, came out from under the tablecloth and rushed at Roland.

Roland tipped the table over to bar the Warrior's way, but the Warrior vaulted it and the fight continued. Roland was deliberately trying to back away to the stairs, but the Warrior kept cutting him off. He used a thick rope to guard himself, but as he ducked away from another aggressive slash, the rope was severed. A large, wooden, cross-type chandelier crashed down, just missing the Warrior!

Roland was beginning to wonder how long he'd be able to keep this up. His superhero spirits were beginning to desert him. He took a deep breath and resumed the toe-to-toe slogging match, with his back to the wall.

They suddenly locked swords, the blades sliding across one another, until Roland's sword became caught in a v-shaped groove in the Warrior's jagged weapon.

The Warrior began twisting it...

Roland feared he would twist the sword out of his grasp. He leaned against the wall, raised his leg and got his foot against the Warrior's chest. With an effort, he managed to thrust him away.

The Warrior fell to the floor, but before Roland could take any advantage, his foe was up again. They now both held their swords two-handed.

The Warrior rushed at Roland and their blades clashed...

To Roland's chagrin, his blade snapped off. He watched the broken blade skimming across the floor and realised he had no choice now but to run for it. He slowed Warrior's advance by throwing the bladeless sword hilt at him, giving himself time to take up a flag banner with a pointed boss to fend the Warrior off.

The Warrior sliced the banner off in pieces, as if he was chopping up a cucumber!

Roland found himself up against the wooden door.

The Warrior levelled his sword like a lance and thrust it at Roland. He meant to finish Roland off...

Roland had other plans. He made a sharp move and dodged to the left. The blade missed him by millimetres, and stuck into the door.

The Warrior struggled to free his sword, giving Roland time to go to another suit of armour and take himself a new sword – and a shield as well.

Roland turned to face his adversary as he backed towards the stairs again.

The Warrior threw a rope around Roland's ankles. It tangled around Roland's legs and tripped him up. He fell just short of the stairs and rolled over and over to unravel himself. He avoided a glancing blow that hit the floor and produced sparks, took one last roll, and was free from the rope. He quickly took up a fighting stance once again, ready for the final act.

The two boys circled each other, making the circle wider and wider, until they were as far apart as they could be. The Warrior was in front of the throne and Roland against the door. The red carpet ran between them as they began a slow approach towards each other along the carpet.

In Roland's mind, the walk took on a slow motion feel, as they stepped closer and closer. It was like the part of a Western movie where two protagonists – the good guy and the bad guy – walk towards each other, down Main Street, for the showdown. They came face to face, glaring at each other from behind their helmets.

'Nobody pass a Warrior!' the Warrior ordered.

'Let me pass,' demanded Roland. He sounded equally confident and convinced of his cause.

'Fight!' said the Warrior.

They clashed again, but it was obvious that both of them were very tired. Their actions took on a slow and deliberate appearance, which became positively lethargic, until they were just trading soft, weary blows. One... after... the... other... Up went the Warrior's sword. Down it came on to Roland's shield. Then Roland's sword came down, parried by the Warrior's sword.

Roland yelled in a hoarse voice, before each blow, 'I want to get –' And then on the blow – *Klaaaang!* – 'Out!'

They carried on, resembling exhausted boxers who were just pummelling each other, neither waiting for the bell. Then, with one almighty effort, the Warrior hit Roland's sword from his grasp.

Roland sank down on one knee, his shield above his head, anticipating a shower of blows from the Warrior.

The Warrior towered above him and raised his sword ready for the *coup de grace*. 'Fight!' he shouted.

Roland moved deftly off the carpet and gave it a tug.

The Warrior, so set on defeating Roland with an almighty blow, lost his balance and found himself toppling over. In an effort to break his fall, he managed to trap his sword underneath himself.

The tables had turned.

Roland retrieved his sword and stood over the Warrior. He held his sword two-handed and pointed it directly at his enemy's heart.

The Warrior glared up at him.

'Give in?' said Roland.

'Never. A Warrior never surrender. You must kill me. You have beaten me, now it is right, it has to be. You must kill me.'

Roland hesitated. He looked into his vanquished foe's imploring eyes.

'I cannot live with shame, no! Kill me! Now! Aaaaaaaarh!' With an echoing cry of utter helplessness, the Warrior began to fade, then disappear completely, leaving nothing but echoes of his despairing cry. Soon that, too, had faded away.

In frustration Roland drove his sword into the stone floor. It went in about eight inches. Roland watched the quivering sword, then wearily took off his helmet.

He heard the sound of slow clapping, coming from the gallery. He turned, and saw Vein standing by the throne, with a sort of self-satisfied grin on his face.

'Go on, boy,' said Vein.

Roland mounted the stairs, to find the gallery apparently empty.

The Lord emerged from the shadows and moved away from Roland.

'No! Wait!' called Roland.

But the Lord kept moving as he spoke. 'Sorry, son. I got a lot of things to do, stuff to listen to. Everything...' He hurried into the shadows again.

'Stop!' cried Roland and ran after him.

The Lord kept up his chatter as he ran from Roland. 'Look, I told you. I can't see you now. Too many things all piling up on top of me. I got this place on my back, round my neck. And what about the music?'

The Lord stopped and looked back at Roland – a look between father and son.

In the silence, they could hear the tinny music issuing from the pots on the crown downstairs.

'What about me?' said Roland. They had gone full circle and reached the stairs again.

The Lord went down the stairs, pursued by Roland. 'I can't solve your problems,' he said.

'You're responsible for them,' Roland said.

The Lord stopped at the bottom of the stairs and turned up to him. 'Oh yeah. I'm responsible for everything, man. But, as of now, I got more important things to do.' He strode away with Roland trailing him.

'But you've got to help me!' said Roland.

The Lord nipped up the steps to the safety of the throne. 'I... have... not!' With that, he put the coronet and pots on. 'Just leave me in peace! Let me get some work done! All you people clamouring round me, demanding this demanding that! You think I asked for this?'

'But I've got to get out!' pleaded Roland. 'Don't you understand?'

'Talk to Vein,' said the Lord, and with that, he became entirely engrossed in the music blasting into his ears. He was lost to the world.

Roland spotted Vein leaning on the sword he'd thrust into the floor. With a last disapproving look at the Lord, he moved over to him. 'Now what?' he asked, looking at the sword. 'After all that! I've gone as far as I can go and it's still no use.'

'What d'you mean boy?' said Vein.

'Got to the top, haven't I?'

'Not quite,' said Vein tantalisingly. He looked from Roland up at the Lord, then slowly back at him. 'Not quite yet.'

Hell, thought Roland. This was Vein up to his stupid tricks again. What more would he have to do to get out? Surely he'd done enough now? Despite his annoyance he said, 'I see.'

Vein nodded at the Lord. 'He's above you, isn't he? He's at the top. Not you. He's standing in your way, blocking your path, impeding your progress. There's one more key boy... One.'

'Give it to me, then,' said Roland bluntly. 'I've earned it, haven't I?'

'Oh yes, beyond all shadow of a doubt.'

'Well then?' Roland held out his hand.

A smile appeared on Vein's face. 'I haven't got it.' He nodded up to the Lord. 'He has! The key to the Castle, boy. Get hold of that, you can do as you like, can't you?'

'How do I get it? said Roland, fearing yet another difficult confrontation.

Vein pulled the sword back, then let it go, and made it swing into Roland's hands. 'You know the old story, don't you?'

Roland looked down, at what he had in his hands. The sword in the stone. When he glanced back at Vein, the old man had disappeared again.

Roland looked at the Lord. It was inevitable, he decided. He drew forth the sword from the stone and raised it.

His Excalibur.

The Lord's eyes were closed. He was 'digging' the music blaring in his ears.

Holding the sword high, Roland approached the Lord.

Chapter Six

Not hear? when noise was everywhere! it toll'd
Increasing like a bell.

ROLAND STALLED and stood in front of the Lord, not knowing how to start things. He decided to go in boldly.

He used the tip of the sword to flip the coronet off the Lord's head, along with the pots, and sent them crashing to the floor.

The Lord was at first startled and then angry. 'What – what you doing to me, man?'

Roland moved the sword to the side, not threatening, but assuring the Lord he had it. 'I want the key,' he said boldly.

The Lord grabbed at the gold chain around his neck. The

key was hidden inside his shirt. 'Key? What d'you want the key for?'

Roland took a breath. No turning back, he thought to himself, no more excuses. This was it. 'To be King of the Castle,' he said.

The Lord looked at Roland, both puzzled and amused at the same time. 'Why do you want to be king?'

'To be free of course,' Roland replied in a steady voice.

The Lord smiled. 'Free?'

'Yes!' Roland's raised voice echoed in the hall.

'Are you sure you know what you're doing?' the Lord asked, shaking his head.

'I think so,' said Roland and then held out his hand. 'The key.' His voice softened, just a little, as he said, 'Please.'

The Lord took off his chain and held it up to Roland, the key swinging before his eyes. Roland noted that the key was in the shape of a turret. It looked very much as if it was made of lead. When Roland took the key, the Lord heaved a sigh of immense relief. Roland, still holding the sword one handed, put the chain around his neck.

'Thank you,' said the Lord. 'From here on, you bear the weight of kingship: an imperious gravity of movement and utterance. I thank you.' With his first sign of sprightliness, the Lord vacated the throne and went down to Roland's level.

They both looked back up the throne.

The Lord grinned at Roland. 'Go on. Try it.'

Roland suddenly began to feel as if he really were royal. He moved up to the dais at a stately pace and plonked himself down on the throne. He found it very much to his liking.

'You like it?' said the Lord.

Roland nodded.

'Good,' said the Lord as he approached Roland with an outstretched hand. 'Well, allow me be the first to congratulate you.'

Roland too stretched out his hand – not to be shaken, to be kissed! He held his palm pointing stiffly down. He recalled how to do this from a film he'd seen, where all the underlings had to show their allegiance to the throne, by kissing the king's hand.

The Lord dutifully lowered his head over Roland's hand and said, 'Your Majesty.'

Bang!

'That's it, he's free now,' shouted Curry, the lift engineer, banging in the cable guide with a four-pound lump-hammer.

Clank!

'The winch, he's free!'

Bong!

This was of course, far, far, away. Maybe, in an antimatter world of a certain kind of reality – but certainly a different reality. Equal but opposite.

'That's it, he's free now!'

Voss was relieved. He watched Hurdle, the chief engineer, approach with a lump of misshapen metal. 'What was it?' he asked.

'Amazin', said Hurdle. 'Piece of lead holdin' it back.' He placed the lead in Voss's hand.

Curry called to his mate, 'Come on then, give us a hand.'

Voss fingered the lead thoughtfully. 'Lead? Shouldn't be any lead.'

Hurdle appealed to Voss, 'Could you give us a hand here?'

Voss was still mulling over the piece of lead. 'Why lead?'

'Er, Mr Voss, d'you mind givin' a hand?'

Voss, still in a thoughtful state, mumbled, 'I'll get someone.'

The two engineers exchanged sour glances.

'Don't want to get his hands dirty, does he?' said Curry.

Voss went downstairs to where the others were waiting. He smiled and nodded. 'We've done it! It's free now, but we need a hand. Long pull to get it up here here.'

Sergeant Tarr held Voss by the arm. 'What was it?'

Voss held up the offending piece of lead. 'Lump of bloody lead, would you believe?'

Roland was sitting on the throne, sword by his side. He examined the key, now hanging from his neck, then lay back in the throne. He had the full swagger of power about him now as he surveyed his domain and he gave a contented sigh. *All mine*, he thought. *But I don't just want a castle. If I'm a king, I want some subjects to govern. They can honour and obey me. Mmm, yes. That sounds right.*

He stirred slowly, as if there were a weight on him.

'Vein!' he called, in his best royal manner.

A few seconds went by. Then there was a click, as the small door at the end of the red carpet opened, and Vein shuffled in, his head averted from the royal gaze. He made a long entrance of it, limping and shuffling up to the foot of the dais, where he genuflected to his new master, one hand trailing the floor – just the slightest bit overdone. 'You called, my liege?'

Roland looked down at Vein, who had his head screwed away from him. 'Look at me, Vein.'

Vein shaded his eyes with his hand. 'Can't do that, Sire. Too majestical bright, you are.'

Roland was a bit miffed when he realised that Vein was mocking him. He put on a more commanding voice. 'I command you, Vein!'

Vein looked at him. 'Then I shall, Sire.' He was as pandering and obsequious as ever. 'Ah, there's King you are... highly regal.'

'That's enough, Vein,' said Roland.

'Sire.' Vein averted his gaze again.

Roland went over his reply a couple of times in his mind before deciding to speak. 'We have decided –'

Vein cheekily looked around for the others included in the 'we'.

'That's *me*, Vein.'

'Ah,' exclaimed Vein.

'– that you shall be made Lord Lieutenant of the Castle.' Roland interrupted himself. 'Look at me, Vein!'

Vein did so.

'And Chief Adviser to ourself –'

At this, Vein gave a silent 'tut!' The boy was at it again, coming over all superior.

'– and Leader of the Privy Council.' King Roland, the King of the Castle, paused to see the effect on Vein. 'Well?'

Vein did yet another cringing over-the-top bow. 'Oh my humble thanks, Sire, most grateful I am. Lord Lieutenant was it? Rest assured, Majesty, I shall prove worthy of the post.'

Roland waved an arm in Vein's general direction and said rather haughtily, 'Mmm. You have been a good servant. It is a just reward.'

'Lord Lieutenant. I never expected that,' Vein said, with a tinge of irony. 'What do I have to do though?'

Roland had no idea. He started to wonder why he'd said it, and tried to think up some sort of job description. 'Well, you have to be... my lieutenant and... sort of... advise me. Yes. And do my bidding, that sort of thing.'

Vein looked straight at Roland and, with a smile flickering on his lips, said gravely, 'Ah, your second in command, like?'

'Yes,' said Roland, pleased that Vein had done his work for him.

Vein pressed him again, 'Next in line, so to speak?'

'What?' Roland was confused, not sure that's what he meant at all.

'Next in line to the throne... After you, that is, Sire.'

Roland decided that Vein was taking some kind of advantage. And after he'd been so generous to him too, he thought crossly. 'One step at a time, Vein,' he said.

Vein bowed even lower. 'Yes, your Majesty, of course, your Majesty.'

Roland nodded, he felt placated. 'Right. First thing, I want to make arrangements to get out.'

'You don't have to do that, Sire. You can leave anytime. Come and go as you like. After all, you are the king.'

'Good.' Roland savoured a real feeling of satisfaction. 'Well, before I do go, I want to see some changes made.'

Vein became suspicious, and turned his eyes away. 'Changes, Sire?'

'Yes. I know what's going on Vein. The waste, stupidity, the chaos. It's criminal, wicked, vicious...'

Vein answered cautiously. 'It all works its own way, they've all got their jobs to do.'

Roland began to remember the hurt, indignation and anger at all the things he'd been through, all the ridiculous states of being that he'd witnessed. He'd had no control over anything, *then*. Now he did...

Roland crossed Vein. 'Little empires, Vein. They're all running their own little empires. There's no co-operation, communication, no proper plan, no direction from above, no purpose. I shall give them that purpose. Before I go, I want this place running like a gold clock!'

'Yes, Sire. Where would you like to start?' said Vein.

In an antechamber of the Great Hall, the Lord was listening to music on his pots – *sans* crown. The door flew open and there stood Roland with Vein beside him.

'Tell him, Vein!' said Roland, imperiously.

'His Majesty said you are to be secretary,' said Vein.

'Me?' replied the Lord.

'You will take note of the changes I make,' Roland said, 'and Vein will see that they're carried out.'

Vein and the Lord glanced at each other behind Roland's back.

'I see,' said the Lord.

Vein grinned and said to the Lord, 'That's it. You and me, working together like...'

In the corridor of cubicles where Roland had first met Voysey, things were going on in their usual way. A muddle of supplicants were waiting around, hoping to see officials.

A door opened in the wall and out marched Roland with Vein and the Lord in tow.

Roland went up to Voysey.

Voysey didn't look up. 'Next!' he shouted.

Vein moved up to him and announced, 'His Majesty the King!' He leaned towards Voysey and spoke, sotto voce, 'Reorganisation, see.'

'Not again,' whispered Voysey.

Vein stepped aside, bowed, and presented King Roland. 'His Royal Majesty.'

Voysey stood up and did a tiny nod of the head.

'These forms, Voysey,' said Roland. He picked up a sheaf of forms and selected one. 'What's this one for?'

'It's, ahh...' Voysey read the heading. He flicked through a few forms then held up another one. 'It's to get this.'

'And what's that for?'

'For the records, and files.'

'Delays!' snapped Roland. 'That's all they create. As I well know, Voysey.' Roland tore the forms in half and threw them on the floor. 'Get rid of them,' he said, in a very majestic manner.

'But the supplicants – what will they do?'

'Send them straight to me.'

'But I shall be... redundant.'

Roland turned on his heel. 'Quite. I want all this burnt.'

Vein turned to the Lord. 'Write down "Burn it."'

Voysey collapsed at his desk, a man with no future.

But when Roland was out of earshot, Vein turned to the sobbing man. 'Don't take it to heart, Mr Voysey. You're not finished yet.'

Voysey looked up at him with hope in his eyes.

Roland descended a long staircase, followed by Vein and the Lord. He opened the door of the Governor's office and strode in. Within moments, he was standing behind the Governor's desk, facing the Governor and the Guard.

'I want these two clapped in irons,' Roland said to Vein.

Vein nodded, then turned to the Lord. 'Write down "clap in irons".'

'But there will be chaos and disruption!' said the Governor, in a very forthright manner. 'I'm warning you!'

'You dare to warn me?' said King Roland. He turned and addressed Vein, to modify his order. 'Heavy irons I think, Vein. Off with them!'

As the Governor and the Guard were taken away, the Lord ushered in the three children: Alfie, Beattie and Delta, all free of their chains.

Roland became more relaxed. 'You see? I've come back.'

'They were going to beat me after you went,' said Alfie.

Roland told Vein, 'This boy is never to be beaten again.'

Vein turned to the Lord. 'Write down "Beaten again".'

Beattie chimed in, 'I knew you'd go and change it all!'

'Enough!' Roland leaned back. 'This one is to go to the Lady of the Castle.'

Beattie looked frightened. 'But I don't know her!'

'You will live in love and affection for ever.'

'But that'll be all different,' protested Beattie.

'Write down "Love and affection,"' Vein instructed the Lord. He pinned a label on Beattie, which had written on it: TO THE LADY OF THE CASTLE. LEV 2.

Roland turned to the last child. 'Delta.'

'Not goin' to take my jewels are you?' she snivelled.

'Yes,' said Roland.

Delta clutched her little bag to her chest. 'You mustn't. They're mine.'

'Listen, Delta. You shall have real jewels, you shall be keeper of the crown jewels.'

Vein said '"Crown jewels,"' and moved closer to the Lord. 'Put a query after that.'

'But I don't want them,' sobbed Delta 'I want *these*. I want to keep these – they're real.'

Roland ignored her wailing and turned to Alfie again. 'Alfie, you and all the other children shall be set free.' He awaited a joyous reaction.

Alfie frowned and mumbled. 'But I don't know what to do if I don't work.'

'Play,' said Roland, with a cheery smile.

'What's that?' said a very confused Alfie.

'You'll find out,' said Roland.

He waved them away and the Lord ushered them out.

The Chef and the Sous Chef entered, looking uncertain about whether to bow or not.

'Ah, welcome from your King,' said Roland.

Then the pair bowed, in a flowery manner, in complete unison.

'Your magnificence,' said the Chef.

Roland said to Vein, 'They are to create their finest dishes for the banquets I shall give.'

'Scusi,' said the cringing Sous Chef.

Vein gave the Lord his note. 'Write down "Catering".'

The Sous Chef again tried to get Roland's attention, 'Scusi.'

But the Chef chimed in before he could speak. 'Thank-a-you, your 'ighness! Grazie, grazie, mille grazie.'

The Sous Chef spoke a little louder this time. 'Scusi your royalness – issa bad snag.'

'What?' said Roland.

'He can't-a-cook. Nor me.'

Roland didn't want to hear any dissent. Orders were orders, he thought, as he swept out of the Governor's office with his retinue – Vein, the Lord, and the two guards escorting their ward, Beattie, who sniffed loudly from time to time to make sure they knew how upset she was.

They all kept a respectful distance behind Roland, who was deep in thought as he paced on to another destination.

They descended more stairs until they reached the level where the Lady's chamber was. Roland opened the door and went in.

When the Lady saw Roland, she immediately spread her arms in welcome. Tears were flooding down her face. 'Oh, my boy, my boy, you've come back! You've come back.'

Roland put on a stern, yet not unfriendly, tone as he moved out of her way. 'No. Not me. But I have brought someone.' Roland gave a flick of his fingers and Beattie was ushered forward. 'For you to... care for.'

The Lady's eyes turned towards Beattie, and her tears moulded into a smile of joy as she looked her up and down. 'Oh my princess! My own! My child – come to me – how pretty you are! Come, eat, drink, rest.'

Roland stepped between them. 'Provided...'

The Lady was all ears...

'Provided that you cease your magical practices immediately. You promise?'

The Lady was confused. 'But how will I bind her to me?' she wondered.

Vein interrupted with heavy sarcasm. 'Endless and unchanging luxury, I should think.' He spoke to Beattie. 'What you want, isn't it girl?'

The Lady hugged Beattie protectively and pulled her away from Vein. She turned to Roland, looked him squarely in the eye, and said solemnly, 'I promise.' She led Beattie away, ecstatic with joy.

Roland gave Vein a supercilious look. 'You see? Another problem solved.'

Vein replied in his usual obsequious manner. 'Yes... Sire.'

As they moved off for another encounter, Roland felt rather pleased with himself. He was setting the world to rights. Even if it *was* the mad, mad, world he was in at that time. He looked forward to going out and breathing fresh clean air again, to catching up with his beloved comic book characters and, well, just getting back to normal.

For a moment, a cloud raced across his mind. The staircase he was on reminded him of a place he once lived in, where danger lurked on the stairs. He saw shadows, dark corners, lights on stair railings, all creating a lattice of fear...

He let the fear slip from his mind. Now, as King, he felt he could easily deal with the problems of that other place. They were problems from a long time ago.

He was a different person now.

Hawkspur's laboratory was silent, except for the ticking of a metronome wagging to and fro. This was suddenly joined by the sound of a toy xylophone tinkling *Three Blind Mice* – badly out-of-tune. The player was Ergon. He was covered in splints and bandages after his fall, and was trying to keep in time, but failing miserably.

Hawkspur, who was listening, suddenly started tearing at his hair. 'No! No! No!' he shouted. He took Ergon's hands in his own and, haltingly, banged out the first notes of the tune. 'One, two, three! Four, five, six! Three, blind, mice. See, how-they, run.'

'I won't,' said Ergon, which in his minimal vocabulary of words seemed to mean, *I see.*

Roland flanked by his escort entered the Laboratory.

'All stand for his Majesty the King,' announced Vein.

'Hawkspur,' called Roland.

Hawkspur peered at them. He recognised Roland. 'You!' he shouted as he approached him. 'You see what you have done?' He indicated the moronic Ergon tinkling away. 'Mn? To my creation. You see? Mn?'

'You tried to steal my voice, Hawkspur,' said Roland.

'It was necessary.'

'Nothing you do is necessary.'

'What?' said Hawkspur. He glared at Roland.

Roland went in harder. 'I am King now. And you will work for the good of the Castle. We have decided that there are too many staircases. You are a scientist, an inventor – invent me a lift system that works.'

'But I create beauty, symmetry, life...'

Roland indicated Ergon. 'Then what is that?'

Hawkspur was hurt. His hand went to his heart and he breathed deeply. He ignored Roland and said, 'Show him, Ergon. Play the tune.'

'I won't!' responded Ergon. He played the three faltering notes, all out of time.

'Stop!' shouted Roland.

One last *ting* and Ergon stopped.

Roland continued, not looking at Hawkspur. 'A lift system, Hawkspur. A fully automatic, hydraulically operated, foolproof lift system.'

The Lord and Vein smirked at one another.

Having carried out a thorough inspection of his realm and suggested several urgently needed reforms, King Roland was seated in the Great Hall, ready to seal the new – and just – laws he had passed.

Blam! Roland slammed the royal seal down on a parchment. He signed beneath it and reached for another one. The whole refectory table was strewn with scrolls of parchment, laid side by side like wallpaper.

As Vein received each one, he tied it with red ribbon, then put it on the table and rolled the others forward.

The Lord, stationed at the other end of the table, collected each scroll as it fell off. He'd gathered a great armful.

Vein approached Roland. 'I hope you don't mind me

jogging your memory, Sire. It's just a thought, like. Wasn't the whole point of you becoming King for you to... get out? Wasn't it, Sire?'

'Yes, I shall, I shall,' replied Roland. 'It is, it was. I haven't forgotten. But I've got to get this done haven't I? I can't leave a job half finished?'

Vein and the Lord exchanged sly smiles.

'What are you two sniggering at?'

Vein nodded towards the Lord and said, 'Tell him.'

'It's that there's a catch, old son, always is, isn't there?'

'What catch?' asked Roland.

'Well,' said the Lord. 'You became King to get out, and now that you're King, you can't get out, because you're too busy being King to get out. Get it?'

'He's right, your Majesty.'

'But I can't leave now. The Castle needs me.'

Vein confronted Roland face on. 'Exactly, Sire. When you came here, you were a boy, a frightened boy – "Childe Roland to the Dark Tower came" – and you fought your way up into a position of power and responsibility. And now, you're trapped.'

Roland mulled this over and replied, 'I know what you're after, Vein.' He banged his fists down on the throne arms. 'This. This is why you want me to go, why you're trying to get rid of me. So that you can sit here, you can rule – that's why, Vein. Want to be King, don't you?'

Vein grinned back at Roland, but didn't answer him. He and the Lord retreated to the antechamber and kept an eye on things through the door, which had been left ajar. They saw Roland, in his thinking pose on the throne, chin resting on arched hands...

*

'Got him going. Crumblin' now. Be crackin' up soon, and then...' Vein smashed his fist into his palm. 'Smash him down!'

'Just your game, Vein, isn't it? Well, this place needs a rat to run it.' With that the Lord put his pots on again.

'Sticks and stones, m'Lord,' said Vein.

But the Lord was already 'gone' on the cool music flowing into his ears. 'Anything you say, Vein.'

Vein went to the crack in the door to observe Roland further. He was watching furtively when Voysey entered from the corridor, highly agitated.

'It's hopeless, absolutely hopeless,' Voysey stuttered.

'What is?' asked Vein.

'There's no proper procedure for anything. I can't ask the King if I can't see the King, can I? Going round in circles. Hopeless.'

Vein brushed Voysey aside and went into the Great Hall.

Roland saw him. 'I want to call a conference, Vein,' he said.

'Yes, Sire,' said Vein, then turned away, with a pained look on his face.

'Well?'

Vein stopped abruptly. 'I was thinking along the same lines myself, Sire. Only I was thinking more in terms of a banquet, Sire... In your honour?'

'Banquet? No time for that.'

'Thinking of more of a sort of *working* banquet, if you know what I mean? Combining business with pleasure... Your Majesty.'

Roland mulled it over in his mind. His thoughts were

mostly concerned with getting things sorted out in the Castle so that he could get going and be free from it all. Goodness, he thought, what a lot there was to do! On the other hand, he *had* been working very hard of late. Maybe a little relaxation would be nice. And, well, the words "in your honour" appealed to him...

He replied to Vein, 'Mn. In my honour? Mn. Very well. See to it, Vein.'

Obsequious as ever, Vein did a foppish circling twist of his hand before bowing low. He backed away, shuffling his feet, right out into the corridor.

In the corridor, Hawkspur waited.

Vein whispered, 'It's all in hand, Doctor. You may resume your own experiments. Can I count on your support?'

Hawkspur nodded.

Vein moved on along the corridor, where he found the Lady. He smiled and approached her. 'I give you my word m'Lady, there will be no ban on magical practices. Are you with me?'

She nodded, gratified.

Vein moved on again to where the Governor was standing. He whispered into his ear.

The Governor's reaction was to smile and nod.

'Then we are agreed?' said Vein and he loped off to where Voysey was standing by his desk, fretting.

He looked up expectantly as Vein approached him.

'It's all settled?' Vein said.

Voysey nodded.

'Then on with the banquet!'

*

In the Great Hall, the table was laid, the silver glittering, and the candelabra lit. Roland was on his throne at the head of the table. Vein, the Lady, Beattie, Delta, Alfie, Voysey and Ergon – who was still in his splints and bandages – sat in the middle. Hawkspur was at the foot. The Governor and the Guard were acting as footmen.

Roland leaned over to Vein, indicating them with a nod. 'Why are they not in chains?'

'Noise, Sire. The clattering creates a bad impression.'

There was a fanfare, and the Chef and the Sous Chef entered, bearing huge silver chafing dishes. The men stood each side of Roland and lifted the lids with a flourish.

Roland examined the contents.

'You like?' asked the Chef, smiling in anticipation of a compliment.

Roland pulled a face. 'It's stew! It's stew and mash!'

The Sous Chef took a ladle full of the stew, ready to dump it onto Roland's plate. 'You like?'

Roland refused the slop.

The others all had their plates loaded up and ate the stuff with relish – almost as if it was some grand dish with a weird French name – but it was the same muck that Roland had seen being doled up in the kitchen.

Roland found it incredible that his guests all finished every last morsel on their plates. He felt aggrieved, but somehow helpless too. There was that familiar nagging feeling of suspicion. It was something to do with Vein's attitude, which came perilously close to being off-hand, insolent even... He watched the last dish being cleared away, then he took charge. 'Right now, your reports. What progress so far, Hawkspur?'

Hawkspur glanced at Vein.

Vein nodded.

Roland was uneasily aware of it.

Hawkspur made a great kerfuffle about getting up and setting his chair. He cleared his throat and said, 'None.'

'None?' said Roland.

'Lifts, Sire, hydraulic or otherwise, are beneath my dignity as a scientist.'

'I see,' said Roland, who was already scenting something in the wind. He looked over at Voysey. 'Voysey?'

'I can't work under these conditions, Sire. Hopeless.'

'My Lady?'

'What is life, without a little magic?' she intoned, her voice heavy with melodrama.

'Beattie?' said Roland.

'Things are changing all the time. That's the trouble.'

'Alfie?'

'I don't like it. The children beat me when we play. Let me go back to work.'

'Delta?'

'They're too heavy, those crown jewels. I want my own jewels back – they're my best.'

'And you, my Lord?'

The Lord waited to listen to a final phrase of the music on his pots. 'Busy, old son, can't you see?' And he was away in his music again, and made no further attempt to listen.

Roland stood up. 'You have all disobeyed me! Me, your *King*! Don't you understand? These reforms are for your own good! And for the good of the Castle!' He pointed at them threateningly. 'You shall be punished, all of you! My laws must be obeyed! If necessary, I am prepared to run this Castle alone. I am warning you...'

Vein started banging his pewter tankard on the table and soon, the others all joined in.

Roland had to shout above the frightening din. 'You shall be consigned to the dungeons – stop that! – to the dungeons. Stop, I say! You'll be locked in the dungeon until you come to your senses!'

Vein made a signal with his hand and the noise stopped dead.

The guards, wielding pikes, rushed into the hall and stood still, awaiting orders.

Vein pointed accusingly at Roland. 'Guards! Arrest this traitor!'

The guards rushed towards Roland.

He made a run for it.

They crossed their pikes to stop him, but he dived and rolled underneath them, making for the door to the antechamber.

'After him!' called Vein. 'I want that key!' He had a serious face suddenly. 'I *must* have that key!'

Roland hurtled through the antechamber, slammed the door, and pushed the chaise behind it. Then he dashed off into the corridor and ran, helter-skelter down the corridor – and then into another one, and another...

In the antechamber, Vein was hurrying the guards to move the chaise. 'Hurry! He must not escape. I must have the key of the Castle. Must have it – to be King!'

Roland was exhausted and out of breath. He had to keep

stopping to gulp more air into his lungs. He reached a staircase and sat down on a step, then heard the sound of running footsteps. He got up and started down the stairs, two at a time.

As he reached the kitchen corridor, he suddenly felt himself slowing down. It was as if he were running in slow motion, but he couldn't understand why. He struggled and tried to go faster, but to no avail. He was unable to alter anything.

The pursuing guards were gaining on him fast...

Roland felt himself slowing down even more. He was almost at a standstill, in a horrific nightmare scenario, not being able to move. The guards were running towards him at a normal speed, but he was still weighed down by the mysterious heaviness. He found that now he couldn't even move his arms or legs, and began to panic. What could it be? He had to get moving!

Then he noticed the key, leaden and shiny, dangling outside his shirt. He was suddenly sure that it was the key holding him back, so he wrenched it off and hurled it to the floor... With the burden of kingship gone, he became fleet of foot once more. He sped off, just as the guards were about to grab him.

The guards rushed over to the key on the floor, then stopped as the lone, limping figure of Vein approached.

Vein bent down and grabbed the key, then held it aloft. 'At last! No more lickin' the boots of the likes of Master Roland. The Castle is mine!'

Roland ran down another staircase and came face to face with the Lady.

She ushered him towards her door. 'In here, my child, in here,' she whispered. 'You'll be safe forever!'

Roland was about to rush in, then he remembered that it had been this door that led to his miniaturisation. He checked himself and looked up.

There behind a grille in the door was a very, very small Beattie, weeping.

Roland pushed the Lady to one side. 'No!' he snapped, then ran on.

The Lady called after him in a sour tone. 'You cannot escape! Cannot!' She turned to Beattie as the guards came charging past her, on the heels of the fleeing Roland. 'You are safe now, my pretty.'

Roland came to another staircase. He remembered it as the one where he and the Warrior had fought their duel. He slowed his pace and proceeded carefully.

As he turned the last spiral, he saw Hawkspur at the bottom and Ergon on the landing between them.

'Seize him Ergon, seize him!' screamed Hawkspur.

Ergon lumbered towards Roland, shouting, 'I won't!'

He began to charge at Roland, who dodged him with ease and, once again, the pathetic Ergon went screaming off the edge, down into darkness. 'I woooooon't!'

Hawkspur rushed to the edge to try and do something. His voice breaking with emotion, he knelt at the bars and looked down into the blackness. 'Ergon. No! No! Not again!'

Roland pushed past the distraught Hawkspur and ran on.

The guards clattered down the steps and got entangled

with the kneeling Hawkspur, who was still calling to his beloved construct, 'Ergon – answer me!'

'I wooooooooooooooooooooooooooooooon't...' called a distant, barely discernible voice.

Roland found himself back in the narrow torch-lit corridor. He was running, looking behind, running on, then looking back again to see if the guards were catching up...

In doing so, he had failed to notice that the walls were closing in on him.

He paused for a final look back for the guards and, as he did so, the walls came together, trapping him tight. No matter how he squirmed, he couldn't move.

Vein appeared. 'You see, boy. I have my own ways through this Castle,' he said.

The guards rushed up to them.

'Here we are then, *Master* Roland,' Vein said. He put a heavy emphasis on the word Master. 'Back where you started. How many times have I told you? Up, always up. Never down. Now look at you.' He hoisted the key, which was now around his neck. 'You had the key in your hand, but you wouldn't go, would you? You had to get ambitious, didn't you?'

Roland, now very contrite, bowed his head and sniffed back a tear. 'Please Vein – let me go. Let me go now. I promise I'll never come back.'

'Go? Not now boy.'

'Why?'

'The trial, boy.'

'What for?'

'Treason!' There was a flicker of a smile on Vein's lips as he said, 'Can't let you go *now*.'

Chapter Seven

I saw them and I knew them all. And yet
Dauntless the slug-horn to my lips I set,
And blew. "Childe Roland to the Dark Tower came."

IN A MORE OR LESS sensible world, on the other side of the inside, work was still going ahead. The engineers had manually hoisted the lift up, and Ron and June were waiting anxiously as the lift doors inched into view.

'There it is then,' said Ron.

June heaved a sigh. 'Oh, thank goodness for that.'

They all crowded round as the lift rose agonisingly slowly then clicked into position.

Vine moved to the lift and pressed the button. 'Here we go.'

They waited for the doors to open. Ron put his arm around June as the doors slid back to reveal... a totally empty lift.

No Roland. Nothing.

'Where is he?' said June, totally nonplussed.

'He's gone,' said Ron.

June turned to Vine accusatively. 'You said you saw him go down,' she said.

'What?' replied Vine, as flabbergasted as all of them.

'Well, he's not in here, is he?' she said, with an edge to her voice.

'Let's have a look,' said Vine.

Sergeant Tarr came rattling down the stairs and spoke directly to PC Briggs. 'What's happened? Is he all right?'

'He's not in there, Sarge,' said PC Briggs.

Sergeant Tarr frowned, worried. 'Must be still down there then, somewhere.'

In the world Roland inhabited now, where strange things happened all the time, things were about to get even stranger.

The Great Hall was made out like a courtroom, with tables and chairs in appropriate positions. The judge was the Governor. He was sitting in the highest position, up on the dais on the throne. The Guard was the clerk, sitting below him. The prosecuting counsel, which was Vein, was to the left of the defence table. The two security men were the ushers at the door.

Roland entered the room from below, and walked slowly up into a barred dock. He looked at the Castle's huge coat of arms on the wall above him, and was greeted by loud whispering from the public gallery – which was made up of all the people Roland had met on his journey, including the kids, supplicants, Chefs and others.

The Clerk cleared his throat loudly. The judge waited for silence, then nodded to the clerk, who nodded to Vein.

'Are you Roland Anthony Wright?' asked Vein.

'Am I?'

Vein disregarded his remark and ploughed on. 'You are charged with the following crimes: common theft, grand larceny, sedition, coercion of minors, forgery, treason and conspiracy.'

'How do you plead?' said the Governor.

'Not guilty! I'm not guilty. I haven't...'

The Governor cut him off. 'Silence in the dock! Call the first witness.'

'Call Doctor Hawkspur,' said Vein gravely.

In Roland's mind, things seemed to be all jumbled up. He heard the usher's voice echoing in the distance: *Call Doctor Hawkspur! – Call Doctor Hawkspur! – Call Doctor Hawkspur!*

The next thing Roland knew, Hawkspur was in the witness box looking daggers at him.

Vein addressed him solemnly, 'Doctor, you are our man of knowledge, are you not?'

'That is correct,' answered Hawkspur.

'A question of a stolen voice, is it not?'

'It is.'

'Is the thief in this courtroom?'

'He is.'

'Be so kind as to point him out.'

'It is he!' said Hawkspur, one finger pointed at Roland.

'That's not true! He tried to steal *my* voice!' said Roland.

'There it is – that's the voice!'

Vein turned to the jury. 'Ladies and gentlemen of the jury, you have heard the accused and seen that he is in blatant possession of the missing voice. Flaunting it before the court.'

Roland felt he must put a stop to this crazy thing. 'I object m'lud!'

'Silence in the dock!'

'Thank you, m'lud,' said Vein. Then to Hawkspur. 'Please tell us why this voice was of such importance?'

'It was for my creation.'

Vein crossed him. 'Let the court see exhibit one.'

The guards brought in Ergon, still in his splints and bandages. A murmur of sympathy came from the spectators as Ergon was led, stumbling, to stand before the bench.

Vein bowed his head in sorrow. 'Who would believe now that this poor creature was once the noblest creation of a brilliant mind? All he lacks is a voice. The voice that *he* – Vein pointed at Roland – 'stole!'

'No, it's not true,' said Roland. 'It's my voice; it *always* has been my voice. They were stealing it from me!'

There was uproar in the court at this outburst.

The Governor banged his gavel. 'Silence! Silence in court!' He nodded to Vein as the noise died down. 'Now, Doctor. I ask you to think most carefully before you answer the next question.'

Vein lowered his voice and said, 'How far... what was the distance... between you and the accused at the moment the theft took place?'

'Seven feet four inches,' stated Hawkspur.

'No more?' said Vein.

'No,' replied Hawkspur.

'No less?'

'No,' came Hawkspur's clear answer.

Vein looked around with the air of having won a major victory and repeated gravely, 'Seven feet four inches.' He sat down with a flourish. 'No further questions.'

Roland was distraught. He was deeply hurt by the injustice of it all. He decided to try some simple logic. Someone was bound to see the truth of it sooner or later. 'Look. How can I steal something that is mine? It's part of me, part of who I am, how can I possibly steal it from somebody else?'

But Vein had his next witness in the box. It was the Lady. She was wearing a black veil and her make-up was tear-streaked on her cheek below it.

'That is not the point at issue,' Vein said. 'The point at issue is that you knowingly alienated this lady's affections. In other words, you have not only broken, but *stolen*, her heart!'

Roland shouted at him, 'No! She tried to trap me, imprison me, steal my heart!'

'Silence in the dock!' ordered the Governor.

Vein continued, 'My Lady, I know how this must grieve a woman of your sensibility, but I must ask you...'

The Lady answered in a soft, subdued tone. 'Yes?'

'When the accused came to you, he seemed to you to be in a – turmoil of emotion?'

She cast her eyes down. 'Yes...'

'But you bade him welcome, did you not?'

'Yes, anyone would.'

'You offered food and drink?' continued Vein.

'Yes, all I had.'

'It was a magical potion!' called Roland.

'Silence!' said the Governor.

'You treated him like... a son?' asked Vein.

'Yes,' she said.

'You are a woman of true compassion, m'lady.'

She hung her head.

'And tell me, what was your reward? Larceny! Grand cardiac larceny, members of the jury,' Vein said, addressing the empty chairs.

Roland butted in again, 'What jury?'

'... upon this helpless woman you see before you.'

The Lady started sobbing.

'Glass of water for the witness,' said the Governor.

Vein took it from the usher and gave it to her. Then Vein said, very solicitously, 'Something you wish to say, m'Lady?'

She sniffed and nodded, then pulled herself together and in a breaking voice said, 'He took everything... everything I had, and left me nothing!' She collapsed.

Vein turned once more to the empty jury. 'See him, see him there, the young blackguard! You see how he tries to intimidate an innocent and terrified child?'

Roland was confused. Child? What child? What did he mean? But when he looked at the witness box, he saw Alfie.

'That's not the same witness!' Roland cried. 'Alfie, I tried to help you!'

Now the Chef and Sous Chef were in the witness box.

'You stole-a my recipe,' accused the Chef.

'You change-a da menu,' said the Sous Chef.

Roland's head was spinning. 'But I...'

Now the witness was Beattie. 'You changed everything!' she spat, with real venom.

'I set you free, Beattie!'

But he was talking to Delta.

'You stole my jewels!'

Roland turned to the Governor. 'The witnesses keep changing; how can I question them?

'Silence in the dock!'

When Roland turned back, Voysey was in the witness box and Vein was next to him.

Voysey shuffled his shoulders, desperate to justify himself. 'It was all on his record. I faced him with deception, he resorted to deceit, and then... and then...' It was all too much for him to bear. 'He destroyed my files, all the documents. He changed the system. There was no procedure any more. It was chaos! Anarchy!' He crumpled under the strain of it all.

Vein faced the Court. 'What we have here is a broken man,' he said. 'Broken by the whim of this miscreant here.' He laid a comforting hand on Voysey's shoulder, then in soft, understanding tones said, 'Mr Voysey. Try to remember.'

'Yes,' said Voysey in a hushed voice.

'The accused. Is he left-handed, do you know?'

Voysey paused before answering. 'Partly, yes.'

'Thank you, Mr Voysey,' said Vein triumphantly.

Roland couldn't stop himself from calling out again. 'Times, places, distances, left handed, right handed! What's that got to do with anything?'

He got the inevitable, 'Silence!' from the Governor.

Vein came in quickly. 'Details boy, where you slipped up.' He again turned to the witness in the box. This time it was the Warrior. Vein approached him. 'Now, did the accused set upon you and, by devious and unfair means, deprive you of your existence?'

'Staircase is a Warrior's!'

'How exactly?'

'Staircase is a Warrior's!'

'I see. What happened?' said Vein, full of concern.

'Staircase is a Warrior's!'

Vein made a theatrical turn to the non-existent jury. 'Ladies and gentlemen...'

'There is no jury!' screamed Roland. 'There is no jury!'

Vein carried on above Roland's shouting. 'You have heard, in detail, from the appointed guardian of the Castle, how he became foully, treacherously, thrust out of existence by the accused, without pity or remorse.' He turned to Roland. 'Your witness.'

Roland addressed the Warrior as if he was an idiot. 'You attack *me*. You *always* attack me...'

But as Roland spoke, the Warrior faded into nothing.

'How can I question him if he's not there?' Roland cried. 'This is a travesty – a travesty of justice!'

'Silence in the dock!' bellowed the Governor.

The Lord was now in the witness box.

Vein began questioning him. 'The sword point was at your throat, was it not?'

'Well...' hummed the Lord.

'It was a case of *coup d'etat*? By *force majeure*?'

'Eh?' said the Lord, frowning.

'He took your crown by force, m'Lord?'

'Sort of.'

'In other words, he usurped our position, and proclaimed himself King.'

'Well...'

Vein was not too happy with the Lord's vague answers. 'Er... Thank you, m'Lord,' he said and addressed the jury-less jury again. 'You have heard how this young upstart' – he pointed out Roland – 'laid this trail of havoc throughout the Castle. How he also stole, robbed, cheated, connived and ultimately committed treason – for what? I will tell you for what: to effect the destruction of all we hold dear. The Castle itself, no less! I call upon you ladies and gentlemen of the jury to deliver a unanimous verdict. Guilty as charged!' Vein seated himself abruptly.

'The defence will present its case,' said the Governor.

All heads swivelled around to Roland. Hard inflexible faces, all seemingly convinced of his guilt. He found it rather unnerving and began to stutter. 'I – I – d – d–' He'd known perfectly what he was going to say before, but it all seemed to be crumbling in his mind. He wanted to tell them what fools and idiots they were, how stupid and brainless, all toeing the party line without even a question. But out came slurred sentences. Nothing seemed to knit together for him. 'I was ah – lost. I – didn't, didn't realise, know where I was...'

Things became worse for him, as a rising murmur of disbelief, hostility and displeasure with his total incompetence started up.

'I didn't – mean,' stuttered Roland. 'I only – I don't know what to say...'

'Is that it? Is that it?' hissed the Governor.

Roland was silent, but an involuntary sob came out of him.

'Whimpering? Snivelling? Is that your defence?'

Silence from Roland.

Silence in the court.

Roland had completely lost his way and floundered about, trying to construct a sentence. He clutched at a straw, hoping they would understand. 'I – I – I was trying to get out! I was trying to get out, that's all – trying to get out!

At that moment, things went black for Roland, and he felt no longer in control of what was happening to him. The courtroom began to fade into darkness as his shouts became louder.

He closed his eyes and suddenly saw himself to be in a narrow tunnel or ventilation system. Stuck and struggling.

He felt a rush of panic, claustrophobia...

He stopped struggling and breathed heavily. He could see a light at the end of the tunnel. He tried moving a little slower, inching his way along towards light, but the tunnel seemed to get narrower as he went, curving slightly upwards and away from him...

In the courtroom, Roland was now shouting loudly, 'Trying to get out!

In the inky black tunnel, Roland, still inching towards the light, was becoming stuck...

'Trying to!' Roland yelled again to the court. 'To... get...'

And he was in the long dark tunnel again...

'... out!' And there was a fleeting image of the court.

Then blackness.

In the buzzing courtroom, Roland was silent as the Governor proceeded to ask for the verdict.

The Governor turned to the empty chairs. 'Ladies and gentlemen of the jury, how do you find the prisoner? Guilty or not guilty?'

There was a huge shout of, 'Guilty!'

Roland swivelled around to see that the jury seats were now filled by all the witnesses. Everyone was shouting 'Guilty!' – including Roland himself! He, too, was shouting 'Guilty!' the loudest of all.

The Governor spoke over the clamour, 'Roland Anthony Wright. You have been found guilty as charged. It is now my solemn duty to pronounce sentence upon you. Do you understand?'

Roland nodded gravely.

'In view of the gravity of your offences, I have no alternative but to impose upon you the heaviest punishment that falls within my power.'

A pregnant pause.

'You are to be taken from this place and... banished!'

A gasp of shock!

Somewhere, a heavy metal door slammed shut.

There was a rattle of chains and Roland, suddenly bound in chains, was led by Vein into a dark room.

The only difference between this room and the dungeon

he'd first found himself in, thought Roland, was that there were two doors.

The other door had a grille.

Vein looked at the door with the grille and then at Roland, with a sort of twisted grin on his face. He took the key from around his neck and unlocked Roland's chains, then offered him the key. 'This is it then, boy. Through there.' He indicated the door with the grille. 'And it's all over. For now.'

'What d'you mean?' said Roland.

'You're banished.'

'You mean I'm free?'

'Free as you'll ever be, yes.'

'How? But that's all I wanted.'

'And you got it. And you learned something, didn't you?'

'What's it all been about, Vein?' begged Roland. He noticed that Vein was beginning to fade.

'*You*, boy!' echoed Vein's voice, just before he disappeared completely. 'See you again. P'raps...'

Before Roland could say anything, Vein had gone.

Roland turned and faced the door with the grille, still hearing Vein's echoing voice in the air: *Up you go, boy. Up, boy! Up... up... up...*

Roland opened the door a crack, and was faced with a howling wind. He pushed harder at the door...

As Roland struggled hard to get out, he found himself in another tunnel. This time, he could see a square of light ahead of him. The light felt different in some way. Closer...

As the tunnel got smaller, he saw a flight of stone steps. He moved up to the source of the light, which was coming through a metal grille above him. He pushed hard on the grille. His hands became filthy with dust and grease, but he kept going until, at last, the grille opened and hinged back away from him.

He realised that he was standing in a pit of some kind. Above him was a very ordinary looking room, lit by a single glass bulb hanging from the ceiling. There were no pitch brands. It was almost... normal.

Roland pulled himself up and out of the pit, to find that he was in the caretaker's cleaning store. It was hardly larger than a broom cupboard, filled with electrical equipment, vacuum cleaners, drums of cleaning materials and coils of wire. To Roland it all had a comforting, ordinary, feeling about it. The cleaning powder was called Vim, there was a bottle labelled Cloros, and a tin of Mansion Polish. It was recognisable, everyday stuff, things that had good honest shapes and functions. Roland touched a mop to make sure it was real. It was.

He turned and closed the grille with a clank.

Only then did Roland allow himself a huge sigh of relief. He opened the door of the cleaning store cautiously, still not quite sure what he might find on the other side – and half expecting some ghoul, or unpleasant misfit from a strange other world.

He left the room, and stopped to take things in. Outside, it was all about ordinary life – traffic noise, kids shouting some way off, and birds twittering. It all seemed slightly amplified, but all the better for that.

Roland checked his hands. They were there all right, a bit grimy with dust and grunge... but it was *real* dust and dirt. For the first time, he ventured to believed he was surely back in the real world – his own, real world – at long last.

He moved into the foyer and saw the sign saying: BRANDON HOUSE. Then he knew for sure that all was well. His journey had brought him back home.

He looked into a window and saw his reflection in it. It all looked quite normal.

Then came the clumpity-clump sound of the caretaker's boots on the stairs. Vine.

Roland turned to face him.

Vine looked shocked. 'Where the devil you been, boy? Got the police an' all here, looking for you.'

'In there,' answered Roland, pointing at the cleaning store.

Vine's eyes narrowed. 'How d'you get in there?'

Some short time later, Roland was in the dining area of the flat. Ranged around him were Sergeant Tarr, Voss, Ron, June and Vine. All were staring at him, as he tried to explain what he'd been through.

He deliberately held back on exactly what he remembered, knowing full well that he wouldn't be believed if he told them. 'It was all dark,' he ventured. 'I don't know...' He flashed a look at Vine. 'I found my own way out. It was all dark. I couldn't see what it was. I crawled and saw this light.' He stopped, shrugged. 'Then I came out.' He finished, and bowed his head.

'My store cupboard, that was,' said Vine.

Voss was looking intently at the building plans. 'Yes, there is something marked here. Old foundations or something. It was all built over.'

Sergeant Tarr butted in, 'Didn't you hear us calling and shouting, son?'

'No,' said Roland honestly. He looked up at them and there, in his mind's eye, for a fleeting moment he saw the faces of the Governor, Vein, Voysey, the Lady and the Lord...

June felt Roland's forehead, to make sure he wasn't running a temperature. 'Are you all right, love?'

Roland nodded, but he wasn't too sure. 'Think so...'

'I think it's rest for you. A long rest.' June led Roland to his bedroom, fussing about as she tried to make sure everything was all right. 'You sure you're warm enough, Roland? Can I get you another blanket or anything?'

'He'll be all right now, love, let him get some sleep,' said Ron, steering June towards the door.

'Goodnight, Dad,' said Roland.

'Night, love,' said June.

Roland replied with, 'Night.'

She put the light out before closing the door.

For some while, Roland savoured the feeling of being in his own room, surrounded by familiar things. He looked over at the half-drawn curtains. They waved slightly in the breeze, and the evening light shone through them.

Their familiarity of everything was pleasant to him as he gazed slowly around the room. He took in his posters on the wall, the Frankenstein monster model, the pile of super-hero comics and, finally, the lump of driftwood on the window shelf. It looked like a rocky towering crag, and now, in silhouette, it began to remind him of those strange Disney-esque Rhine castles...

As Roland's eyes closed, somewhere deep down in the block of flats, there was a *Boom!*

The sound of a huge castle door being slammed shut.

Bells were ringing out all along the corridor. Roland was back at school and it was the start of morning lessons. Pupils rushed around, chattering and complaining, as they made their way to their classes.

Roland and three other defaulters were standing outside the music room door waiting, music in hand for last minute learning.

The bells stopped abruptly. After a slamming of doors, the noise in the corridor vanished and there was silence. Then, the door of the music room opened and the frame was filled by Spurgeon in his gown, arms akimbo. Hawker hovered behind him in an identical stance, like a vertical shadow.

Spurgeon cast his eye along the line, then pointed at Roland. 'You, boy. You first.'

'Me, sir?'

'Yes, boy, you. The comic book expert, is it not? Mn?'

As Roland went into the room, Hawker took up his position at the piano and began playing the introduction to Roland's solo piece.

Roland did not sing at the appointed moment.

Hawker started the introduction once more, but Spurgeon waved for him to stop. He spoke in ominously soft tones. 'Why aren't you singing, Wright?'

'Don't know, sir,' came Roland's clear reply.

'Don't you know it?'

'Haven't learned it, sir.'

'Why not?'

'Haven't had the time, sir.'

'Too busy reading? Comics I suppose?' sneered Spurgeon.

'No, sir.'

'Explain yourself, Wright.'

'What, sir?'

'Why you didn't have time?'

Roland took a breath. He was feeling quite relaxed, with not a qualm in him, as he prepared to tell Spurgeon the truth. 'I got into a fight sir. They tore my music up, then I got stuck in a lift, sir.'

'This had better be the truth, Wright.'

There was almost a smile on his lips as Roland said, 'Ask the police if you don't believe me.'

Hawker sensed that Roland was pushing a little too far. 'Steady on now Wright, steady on.'

'Can I tell you something else... sir?'

'Proceed,' said Spurgeon.

'I'm leaving the choir, sir. I'm not learning anything, so it's pointless, sir.'

A silence.

Then Spurgeon cleared his throat. 'Well surely that's for us to decide. Mn?'

'I don't think so, sir. After all, it's my voice.'

Roland was taking the long walk across the muddied grass and stunted trees that formed the grass apron of the flats.

A small figure joined him and kept a step or two behind him. It was Alf.

'Ripper Dobbs got to go to court,' said Alf.

'Has he?' said Roland.

They walked on in silence to the foyer.

'You gettin' a gang up?' said Alf hopefully.

Roland turned back to look at the small boy as he went through the door. 'I've already got my gang,' he said as he moved into the lobby.

Alf was still at the door. 'Who's in it?' he shouted.

Roland called back over his shoulder, 'I am.'

Vine intercepted Roland as he came to the lifts and stairwell. He nodded towards Alf. 'He tell you about "Ripper" did he?'

Roland nodded.

'Hope he gets Borstal. Get some decent people in here. People with a bit of respect for the man in authority. The man with the keys.' He jangled them at Roland. 'Eh?'

Roland put his foot on the stairs.

'Hey,' called Vine.

Roland went on up the stairs.

Vein looked up after him, his face twisted and vengeful. 'We want to break that mob see, smash 'em!'

On the tenth floor, Roland climbed the last few stairs on to the landing. He found Ripper there – alone and not so menacing.

'We got somethin' to settle, Sunbeam,' Ripper said.

Roland showed no fear. 'Have we?' he asked, and looked around. 'Where's your mates, then?'

'You got me in bother.'

'Did I?'

'Yeah, you did. Gotta go to court.'

'So?'

'You haven't, have you? Got off with a caution, didn't ya?' Ripper put on a whiney voice and moved step by step nearer to Roland. 'Because he wears a fancy blazer. Goes to a poncey school. Sings in a dafty choir. An' gets his daddy to take him down the cop-shop.' He was eye to eye with Roland, who hadn't moved an inch away from him. 'Beause he's gutless.'

There was a pause as they stared at each other.

Roland said, 'Am I?' He put his hand into his blazer pocket and a pointed shape appeared. Now Roland advanced on Ripper. 'What d'you think this is in my pocket then?'

Ripper had backed up to the stairs.

Roland made a move.

Ripper stepped back again and hit the bottom stair. He fell and sat down hard on the stairs with an 'Ow!'

Roland stood over the fallen boy, hand still in his pocket.

As Ripper cowered back, his henchmen and the two girls appeared, as if from nowhere. 'Get 'im lads!' he shouted.

His henchmen didn't move.

Roland looked from the gang to Ripper. 'Still want a fight?' he asked.

'Oooh, me back!' moaned Ripper, obviously feigning more pain than he felt.

'I thought you liked fighting, Ripper? But you don't, do you? You like frightening people, that's all,' said Roland.

'Let me get up,' said Ripper.

'Ask properly,' was Roland's retort.

'Let me up...' Ripper had to convince himself to say the last word. 'Please.'

Roland stepped back. 'All right, carry on.'

Ripper got up and went past Roland, but he made no move against him.

It was down to Betty to rally the troops. 'Oh come on!' she called, and they all mooched off.

Ripper turned back to Roland. 'Hey, hang about.'

'What d'you want,' said Della.

Ripper said nothing. He watched Alf follow Roland upstairs, then called out, 'What you got in your pocket then? Show me!'

Roland smiled back at him in answer, then went on up the stairs, his hand still on his pocket. He reached his flat door, put his hand into his pocket and pulled out a key, which had a large tower shape as a fob. The key to his flat.

He put it in the lock.

In his bedroom, Roland was stuffing his old toys and things into a black plastic rubbish bag. All the posters on the walls had been taken down and the furniture moved about.

Ron came in. 'What's all this?' he grinned. 'Not moving out, are you?'

'Getting rid of some old rubbish. Changing it a bit.'

'Er... Son? No trouble was there? On the stairs?'

Roland didn't reply immediately.

'Role?'

'No,' Roland answered brightly.

'Ah, that's good then. Right.' Ron started to move away.

'Dad?' said Roland.

'Yeah?'

'Can you...' He hesitated, then plunged in. 'Can you call me Roland?'

'Oh. Why?'

'Well,' he grinned. 'That's who I am.'

Ron was a bit mystified, taken aback. He went on backing out of the room. 'Yeah... all right. If that's what you want. Fine by me.' He watched Roland doing his clearing up for a few more seconds, and then quietly closed the door.

Roland looked at the closed door and felt a great relief that he'd settled things. He had a tingle of pleasure at the way things were beginning to pan out.

He did a forward roll on to his bed in its new position, and looked around the bare walls...

Satisfied.